**James Baik**

# Through the Telescope

# James Baikie

# Through the Telescope

1st Edition | ISBN: 978-3-75235-096-8

Place of Publication: Frankfurt am Main, Germany

Year of Publication: 2020

Outlook Verlag GmbH, Germany.

# THROUGH THE TELESCOPE

## BY

# JAMES BAIKIE

# PREFACE

The main object of the following chapters is to give a brief and simple description of the most important and interesting facts concerning the heavenly bodies, and to suggest to the general reader how much of the ground thus covered lies open to his personal survey on very easy conditions. Many people who are more or less interested in astronomy are deterred from making practical acquaintance with the wonders of the heavens by the idea that these are only disclosed to the possessors of large and costly instruments. In reality there is probably no science which offers to those whose opportunities and means of observation are restricted greater stores of knowledge and pleasure than astronomy; and the possibility of that quickening of interest which can only be gained by practical study is, in these days, denied to very few indeed.

Accordingly, I have endeavoured, while recounting the great triumphs of astronomical discovery, to give some practical help to those who are inclined to the study of the heavens, but do not know how to begin. My excuse for venturing on such a task must be that, in the course of nearly twenty years of observation with telescopes of all sorts and sizes, I have made most of the mistakes against which others need to be warned.

The book has no pretensions to being a complete manual; it is merely descriptive of things seen and learned. Nor has it any claim to originality. On the contrary, one of its chief purposes has been to gather into short compass the results of the work of others. I have therefore to acknowledge my indebtedness to other writers, and notably to Miss Agnes Clerke, Professor Young, Professor Newcomb, the late Rev. T. W. Webb, and Mr. W. F. Denning. I have also found much help in the *Monthly Notices* and *Memoirs* of the Royal Astronomical Society, and the *Journal* and *Memoirs* of the British Astronomical Association.

The illustrations have been mainly chosen with the view of representing to the general reader some of the results of the best modern observers and instruments; but I have ventured to reproduce a few specimens of more commonplace work done with small telescopes. I desire to offer my cordial thanks to those who have so kindly granted me permission to reproduce illustrations from their published works, or have lent photographs or drawings for reproduction—to Miss Agnes Clerke for Plates XXV.-XXVIII. and XXX.-XXXII. inclusive; to Mrs. Maunder for Plate VIII.; to M. Loewy, Director of the Paris Observatory, for Plates XI.-XIV. and Plate XVII.; to Professor E. B. Frost, Director of the Yerkes Observatory, for Plates I., VII., XV., and XVI.; to M. Deslandres, of the Meudon Observatory, for Plate IX., and the gift of several of his own solar memoirs; to the Astronomer Royal for England, Sir W. Mahony Christie, for Plate V.; to Mr. H. MacEwen for the drawings of Venus, Plate X.; to the Rev. T. E. R. Phillips for those of Mars and Jupiter, Plates XX. and XXII.; to Professor Barnard for that of Saturn, Plate XXIV., reproduced by permission from the *Monthly Notices* of the Royal Astronomical Society; to Mr. W. E. Wilson for Plates XXIX. and XXXII.; to Mr. John Murray for Plates XVIII. and XIX.; to the proprietors of *Knowledge* for Plate VI.; to Mr. Denning and Messrs. Taylor and Francis for Plate III. and Figs. 6 and 20; to the British Astronomical Association for the chart of Mars, Plate XXI., reproduced from the *Memoirs*; and to Messrs. T. Cooke and Sons for Plate II. For those who wish to see for themselves some of the wonders and beauties of the starry heavens the two Appendices furnish a few specimens chosen from an innumerable company; while readers who have no desire to engage in practical work are

# CHAPTER I

## THE TELESCOPE—HISTORICAL

The claim of priority in the invention of this wonderful instrument, which has so enlarged our ideas of the scale and variety of the universe, has been warmly asserted on behalf of a number of individuals. Holland maintains the rights of Jansen, Lippershey, and Metius; while our own country produces evidence that Roger Bacon had, in the thirteenth century, 'arrived at theoretical proof of the possibility of constructing a telescope and a microscope' and that Leonard Digges 'had a method of discovering, by perspective glasses set at due angles, all objects pretty far distant that the sun shone on, which lay in the country round about.'

All these claims, however, whether well or ill founded, are very little to the point. The man to whom the human race owes a debt of gratitude in connection with any great invention is not necessarily he who, perhaps by mere accident, may stumble on the principle of it, but he who takes up the raw material of the invention and shows the full powers and possibilities which are latent in it. In the present case there is one such man to whom, beyond all question, we owe the telescope as a practical astronomical instrument, and that man is Galileo Galilei. He himself admits that it was only after hearing, in 1609, that a Dutchman had succeeded in making such an instrument, that he set himself to investigate the matter, and produced telescopes ranging from one magnifying but three diameters up to the one with a power of thirty-three with which he made his famous discoveries; but this fact cannot deprive the great Italian of the credit which is undoubtedly his due. Others may have anticipated him in theory, or even to a small extent in practice, but Galileo first gave to the world the telescope as an instrument of real value in research.

The telescope with which he made his great discoveries was constructed on a principle which, except in the case of binoculars, is now discarded. It consisted of a double convex lens converging the rays of light from a distant object, and of a double concave lens, intercepting the convergent rays before they reach a focus, and rendering them parallel again (Fig. 1). His largest instrument, as already mentioned, had a power of only thirty-three diameters, and the field of view was very small. A more powerful one can now be obtained for a few shillings, or constructed, one might almost say, for a few pence; yet, as Proctor has observed: 'If we regard the absolute importance of the discoveries effected by different telescopes, few, perhaps, will rank higher than the little tube now lying in the Tribune of Galileo at Florence.'

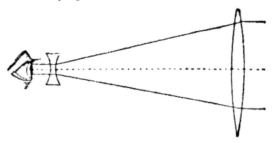

FIG. 1.—PRINCIPLE OF GALILEAN TELESCOPE.

Galileo's first discoveries with this instrument were made in 1610, and it was not till nearly half a century later that any great improvement in telescopic construction was effected. In the middle of the seventeenth century Scheiner and Huygens made telescopes on the principle, suggested by Kepler, of using two double convex lenses instead of a convex and a concave, and the modern refracting telescope is still constructed on essentially the same principle, though, of course, with many minor modifications (Fig. 2).

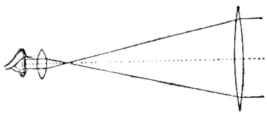

FIG. 2.—PRINCIPLE OF COMMON REFRACTOR.

The latter part of the seventeenth century witnessed the introduction of telescopes on this principle of the most amazing length, the increase in length being designed to minimize the imperfections which a simple lens exhibits both in definition and in colour. Huygens constructed one such telescope of 123 feet focal length, which he presented to the Royal Society of London; Cassini, at Paris, used instruments of 100 and 136 feet; while Bradley, in 1722, measured the diameter of Venus with a glass whose focal length was 212¼ feet. Auzout is said to have made glasses of lengths varying from 300 to 600 feet, but, as might have been expected, there is no record of any useful observations having ever been made with these monstrosities. Of course, these instruments differed widely from the compact and handy telescopes with which we are now familiar. They were entirely without tubes. The object-glass was fastened to a tall pole or to some high building, and was painfully manœuvred into line with the eye-piece, which was placed on a support near the ground, by means of an arrangement of cords. The difficulties of observation with these unwieldy monsters must have been of the most exasperating type, while their magnifying power did not exceed that of an ordinary modern achromatic of, perhaps, 36 inches focal length. Cassini, for instance, seems never to have gone beyond a power of 150 diameters, which might be quite usefully employed on a good modern 3-inch refractor in good air. Yet with such tools he was able to discover four of the satellites of Saturn and that division in Saturn's ring which still bears his name. Such facts speak volumes for the quality of the observer. Those who are the most accustomed to use the almost perfect products of modern optical skill will have the best conception of, and the profoundest admiration for, the limitless patience and the wonderful ability which enabled him to achieve such results with the very imperfect means at his disposal.

The clumsiness and unmanageableness of these aerial telescopes quickly reached a point which made it evident that nothing more was to be expected of them; and attempts were made to find a method of combining lenses, which might result in an instrument capable of bearing equal or greater magnifying powers on a much shorter length. The chief hindrance to the efficiency of the refracting telescope lies in the fact that the rays of different colours which collectively compose white light cannot be brought to one focus by any single lens. The red rays, for example, have a different focal length from the blue, and so any lens which brings the one set to a focus leaves a fringe of the other outstanding around any bright object.

In 1729 Mr. Chester Moor Hall discovered a means of conquering this difficulty, but his results were not followed up, and it was left for the optician John Dollond to rediscover the principle some twenty-five years later. By making the object-glass of the telescope double, the one lens being of crown and the other of flint glass, he succeeded in obtaining a telescope which gave a virtually colourless image.

This great discovery of the achromatic form of construction at once revolutionized the art of telescope-making. It was found that instruments of not more than 5 feet focal length could be constructed, which infinitely surpassed in efficiency, as well as in handiness, the cumbrous tools which Cassini had used; and Dollond's 5-foot achromatics, generally with object-glasses of 3¾ inches diameter, represented for a considerable time the acme of optical excellence. Since the time of Dollond, the record of the achromatic refractor has been one of continual, and, latterly, of very rapid progress. For a time much hindrance was experienced from the fact that it proved exceedingly difficult to obtain glass discs of any size whose purity and uniformity were sufficient to enable them to pass the stringent test of optical performance. In the latter part of the eighteenth century, a 6-inch glass was considered with feelings of admiration, somewhat similar to those with which we regard the Yerkes 40-inch to-day; and when, in 1823, the Dorpat refractor of 9⁶/₁₀ inches was mounted (Fig. 3), the astronomical world seemed to have the idea that something very like finality had been reached. The Dorpat telescope proved, however, to be only a milestone on the path of progress. Before very long it was surpassed by a glass of 12 inches diameter, which Sir James South obtained from Cauchoix of Paris, and which is now mounted in the Dunsink Observatory, Dublin. This, in its turn, had to give place to the fine instruments of 14·9 inches which were figured by Merz of Munich for the Pulkowa and Cambridge (U.S.A.) Observatories; and then there came a pause of a few years, which was broken by Alvan Clark's completion of an 18½-inch, an instrument which earned its diploma, before ever it left the workshop of its constructor, by the discovery of the companion to Sirius.

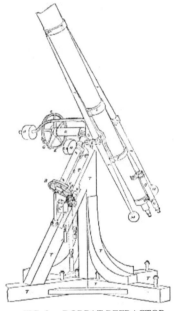

FIG. 3.—DORPAT REFRACTOR.

The next step was made on our side of the Atlantic, and proved to be a long and notable one, in a sense definitely marking out the boundary line of the modern era of giant refractors. This was the completion, by Thomas Cooke, of York, of a 25-inch instrument for the late Mr. Newall. It did not retain for long its pride of place. The palm was speedily taken back to America by Alvan Clark's construction of the 26-inch of the Washington Naval Observatory, with which Professor Asaph Hall discovered in 1877 the two satellites of Mars. Then came Grubb's 27-inch for Vienna; the pair of 30-inch instruments, by Clark and Henry respectively, for Pulkowa (Fig. 4) and Nice; and at last the instrument which has for a number of years been regarded as the finest example of optical skill in the world, the 36-inch Clark refractor of the Lick Observatory, California. Placed at an elevation of over 4,000 feet, and in a climate exceptionally well suited for astronomical work, this fine instrument has had the advantage of being handled by a very remarkable succession of brilliant observers, and has, since its completion, been looked to as a sort of court of final appeal in disputed questions. But America has not been satisfied even with such an instrument, and the 40-inch Clark refractor of the Yerkes Observatory is at present the last word of optical skill so far as achromatics are concerned (Frontispiece). It is not improbable that it may also be the last word so far as size goes, for the late Professor Keeler's report upon its performance implies that in this splendid telescope the limit of practicable size for object-glasses is being approached. The star images formed by the great lens show indications of slight flexure of the glass under its own weight as it is turned from one part of the sky to another. It would be rash, however, to say that even this difficulty will not be overcome. So many obstacles, seemingly insuperable, have vanished before the astronomer's imperious demand for 'more light,' and so many great telescopes, believed in their day to represent the absolute culmination of the optical art, are now mere commoners in the ranks where once they were supreme, that it may quite conceivably prove that the great Yerkes refractor, like so many of its predecessors, represents only a stage and not the end of the journey.

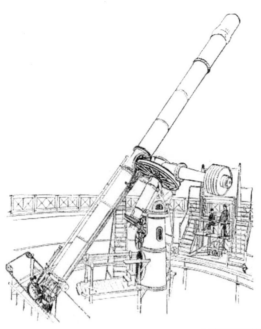

FIG. 4.—30-INCH REFRACTOR, PULKOWA OBSERVATORY.

Meanwhile, Sir Isaac Newton, considering, wrongly as the sequel showed, that 'the case of the refractor was desperate,' set about the attempt to find out whether the reflection of light by means of suitably-shaped mirrors might not afford a substitute for the refractor. In this attempt he was successful, and in 1671 presented to the Royal Society the first specimen, constructed by his own hands, of that form of reflecting telescope which has since borne his name. The principle of the Newtonian reflector will be easily grasped from Fig. 5. The rays of light from the object under inspection enter the open mouth of the instrument, and passing down the tube are converged by the concave mirror AA towards a focus, before reaching which they are intercepted by the small flat mirror BB, placed at an angle of 45 degrees to the axis of the tube, and are by it reflected into the eye-piece E which is placed at the side of the instrument. In this construction, therefore, the observer actually looks in a direction at right angles to that of the object which he is viewing, a condition which seems strange to the uninitiated, but which presents no difficulties in practice, and is found to have several advantages, chief among them the fact that there is no breaking of one's neck in the attempt to observe objects near the zenith, the line of vision being always horizontal, no matter what may be the altitude of the object under inspection. Other forms of reflector have been devised, and go by the names of the Gregorian, the Cassegrain, and the Herschelian; but the Newtonian has proved itself the superior, and has practically driven its rivals out of the field, though the Cassegrain form has been revived in a few instances of late years, and is particularly suited to certain forms of research.

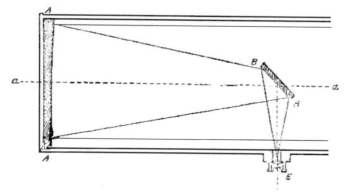

FIG. 5.—PRINCIPLE OF NEWTONIAN REFLECTOR.

FIG. 6.—LORD ROSSE'S TELESCOPE.

At first the mirrors of reflecting telescopes were made of an alloy known as speculum metal, which consisted of practically 4 parts of copper to 1 of tin; but during the last half-century this metal has been entirely superseded by mirrors made of glass ground to the proper figure, and then polished and silvered on the face by a chemical process. To the reflecting form of construction belong some of the largest telescopes in the world, such as the Rosse 6-foot (metal mirrors), Fig. 6, the Common 5-foot (silver on glass), the

Melbourne 4-foot (metal mirrors, Cassegrain form), and the 5-foot constructed by Mr. Ritchey for the Yerkes Observatory. Probably the most celebrated, as it was also the first of these monsters, was the 4-foot telescope of Sir William Herschel, made by himself on the principle which goes by his name. It was used by him to some extent in the discoveries which have made his name famous, and nearly everyone who has ever opened an astronomical book is familiar with the engraving of the huge 40-foot tube, with its cumbrous staging, which Oliver Wendell Holmes has so quaintly celebrated in 'The Poet at the Breakfast Table' (Fig. 7).

FIG. 7.—HERSCHEL'S 4-FOOT REFLECTOR.

# CHAPTER II

## THE TELESCOPE—PRACTICAL

Having thus briefly sketched the history of the telescope, we turn now to consider the optical means which are most likely to be in the hands or within the reach of the beginner in astronomical observation. Let us, first of all, make the statement that any telescope, good, bad, or indifferent, is better than no telescope. There are some purists who would demur to such a statement, who make the beginner's heart heavy with the verdict that it is better to have no telescope at all than one that is not of the utmost perfection, and, of course, of corresponding costliness, and who seem to believe that the performance of an inferior glass may breed disgust at astronomy altogether. This is surely mere nonsense. For most amateurs at the beginning of their astronomical work the question is not between a good telescope and an inferior one, it is between a telescope and no telescope. Of course, no one would be so foolish as willingly to observe with an inferior instrument if a better could be had; but even a comparatively poor glass will reveal much that is of great interest and beauty, and its defects must even be put up with sometimes for the sake of its advantages until something more satisfactory can be obtained. An instrument which will show fifty stars where the naked eye sees five is not to be despised, even though it may show wings to Sirius that have no business there, or a brilliant fringe of colours round Venus to which even that beautiful planet can lay no real claim. Galileo's telescope would be considered a shockingly bad instrument nowadays; still, it had its own little influence upon the history of astronomy, and the wonders which it first revealed are easily within the reach of anyone who has the command of a shilling or two, and, what is perhaps still more important, of a little patience. The writer has still in his possession an object-glass made out of a simple single eyeglass, such as is worn by Mr. Joseph Chamberlain. This, mounted in a cardboard tube with another single lens in a sliding tube as an eye-piece, proved competent to reveal the more prominent lunar craters, a number of sunspots, the phases of Venus, and the existence, though not the true form, of Saturn's ring. Its total cost, if memory serve, was one shilling and a penny. Of course it showed, in addition, a number of things which should not have been seen, such as a lovely border of colour round every bright object; but, at the same time, it gave a great deal more than thirteen pence worth of pleasure and instruction.

Furthermore, there is this to be said in favour of beginning with a cheap and inferior instrument, that experience may thus be gained in the least costly fashion. The budding astronomer is by nature insatiably curious. He wants to know the why and how of all the things that his telescope does or does not do. Now this curiosity, while eminently laudable in itself, is apt in the end to be rather hard upon his instrument. A fine telescope, whatever its size may be, is an instrument that requires and should receive careful handling; it is easily damaged, and costly to replace. And therefore it may be better that the beginner should make his earlier experiments, and find out the more conspicuous and immediately fatal of the many ways of damaging a telescope, upon an instrument whose injury, or even whose total destruction, need not cause him many pangs or much financial loss.

It is not suggested that a beginning should necessarily be made on such a humble footing as that just indicated. Telescopes of the sizes mainly referred to in these pages—*i.e.*, refractors of 2 or 3 inches aperture, and reflectors of 4½ to 6 inches—may frequently be picked up second-hand at a very moderate figure indeed. Of course, in these circumstances the purchaser has to take his chance of defects in the instrument, unless he can arrange for a trial of it, either by himself, or, preferably, by a friend who has some experience; yet even should the glass turn out far from perfect, the chances are that it will at least be worth the small sum paid for it. Nor is it in the least probable, as some writers seem to believe, that the use of an inferior instrument will disgust the student and hinder him from prosecuting his studies. The chances are that it will merely create a desire for more satisfactory optical means. Even a skilled observer like the late Rev. T. W. Webb had to confess of one of his telescopes that 'much of its light went the wrong way'; and yet he was able to get both use and pleasure out of it. The words of a well-known English amateur observer may be quoted. After detailing his essays with glasses of various degrees of imperfection Mr. Mee remarks: 'For the intending amateur I could wish no other experience than my own. To commence with a large and perfect instrument is a mistake; its owner cannot properly appreciate it, and in gaining experience is pretty sure to do the glass irreparable injury.'

Should the beginner not be willing or able to face the purchase of even a comparatively humble instrument, his case is by no means desperate, for he will find facilities at hand, such as were not thought of a few years ago, for the construction of his own telescope. Two-inch achromatic object-glasses, with suitable lenses for the making up of the requisite eye-pieces, are to be had for a few shillings, together with cardboard tubes of sizes suitable for fitting up the instrument; and such a volume as Fowler's 'Telescopic Astronomy' gives complete directions for the construction of a glass which is capable of a wonderful amount of work in proportion to its cost. The substitution of metal tubes for the cardboard ones is desirable, as metal will be found to be much more satisfactory if the instrument is to be much used. The observer, however, will not long be satisfied with such tools as these, useful though they may be. The natural history of amateur astronomers may be summed up briefly in the words 'they go from strength to strength.' The possessor of a small telescope naturally and inevitably covets a bigger one; and when the bigger one has been secured it represents only a stage in the search for one bigger still, while along with the desire for increased size goes that for increased optical perfection. No properly constituted amateur will be satisfied until he has got the largest and best instrument that he has money to buy, space to house, and time to use.

Let us suppose, then, that the telescope has been acquired, and that it is such an instrument as may very commonly be found in the hands of a beginner—a refractor, say, of 2, 2½, or 3 inches aperture (diameter of object-glass). The question of reflectors will fall to be considered later. Human nature suggests that the first thing to do with it is to unscrew all the screws and take the new acquisition to pieces, so far as possible, in order to examine into its construction. Hence many glasses whose career of usefulness is cut short before it has well begun. 'In most cases,' says Webb, 'a screw-driver is a dangerous tool in inexperienced hands'; and Smyth, in the Prolegomena to his 'Celestial Cycle,' utters words of solemn warning to the 'over-handy gentlemen who, in their feverish anxiety for meddling with and making instruments, are continually tormenting them with screw-drivers, files, and what-not.' Unfortunately, it is not only the screw-driver that is dangerous; the most deadly danger to the most delicate part of the telescope lies in the unarmed but inexperienced hands themselves. You may do more irreparable damage to the object-glass of your telescope in five minutes with your fingers than you are likely to do to the rest of the instrument in a month with a screw-driver. Remember that an object-glass is a work of art, sometimes as costly as, and always much more remarkable than, the finest piece of jewellery. It may be unscrewed, *carefully*, from the end of its tube and examined. Should the examination lead to the detection of bubbles or even scratches in the glass (quite likely the latter if the instrument be second-hand), these need not unduly vex its owner's soul. They do not necessarily mean bad performance, and the amount of light which they obstruct is very small, unless the case be an extreme one. But on no account should the two lenses of the object-glass itself be separated, for this will only result in making a good objective bad and a bad one worse. The lenses were presumably placed in their proper adjustment to one another by an optician before being sent out; and should their performance be so unsatisfactory as to suggest that this adjustment has been disturbed, it is to an optician that they should be returned for inspection.

The glass may, of course, be carefully and gently cleaned, using either soft chamois leather, or preferably an old silk handkerchief, studiously kept from dust; but the cleaning should never amount to more than a gentle sweeping away of any dust which may have gathered on the surface. Rubbing is not to be thought of, and the man whose telescope has been so neglected that its object-glass needs rubbing should turn to some other and less reprehensible form of mischief. For cleaning the small lenses of the eye-pieces, the same silk may be employed; Webb recommends a piece of blotting-paper, rolled to a point and aided by breathing, for the edges which are awkward to get at. Care must, of course, be taken to replace these lenses in their original positions, and the easiest way to ensure this is to take out only one at a time. In replacing them, see that the finger does not touch the surface of the glass, or the cleaning will be all to do over again.

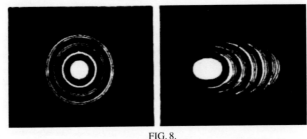

FIG. 8.

*a*, O.G. in perfect adjustment; *b*, O.G. defectively centred.

Next comes the question of testing the quality of the objective. (The stand is meanwhile assumed, but will be spoken of later.) Point the telescope to a star of about the third magnitude, and employ the eye-piece of highest power, if more than one goes with the instrument—this will be the shortest eye-piece of the set. If the glass be of high quality, the image of the star will be a neat round disc of small size, surrounded by one or two thin bright rings (Fig. 8, *a*). Should the image be elliptical and the rings be thrown to the one side (Fig. 8, *b*), the glass may still be quite a good one, but is out of square, and should be readjusted by an optician. Should the image be irregular and the rings broken, the glass is of inferior quality, though it may still be serviceable enough for many purposes. Next throw the image of the star out of focus by racking the eye-piece in towards the objective, and then repeat the process by racking it again out of focus away from the objective. The image will, in either case, expand into a number of rings of light, and these rings should be truly circular, and should present precisely the same appearance at equal distances within and without the focus. A further conception of the objective's quality may be gained by observing whether the image of a star or the detail of the moon or of the planets comes sharply to a focus when the milled head

15

for focussing is turned. Should it be possible to rack the eye-tube in or out for any distance without disturbing the distinctness of the picture to any extent, then the glass is defective. A good objective will admit of no such range, but will come sharply up to focus, and as sharply away from it, with any motion of the focussing screw. A good glass will also show the details of a planet like Saturn, such as are within its reach, that is, with clearness of definition, while an inferior one will soften all the outlines, and impart a general haziness to them. The observer may now proceed to test the colour correction of his objective. No achromatic, its name notwithstanding, ever gives an absolutely colourless image; all that can be expected is that the colour aberration should have been so far eliminated as not to be unpleasant. In a good instrument a fringe of violet or blue will be seen around any bright object, such as Venus, on a dark sky; a poor glass will show red or yellow. It is well to make sure, however, should bad colour be seen, that the eye-piece is not causing it; and, therefore, more than one eye-piece should be tried before an opinion is formed. Probably more colour will be seen at first than was expected, more particularly with an object so brilliant as Venus. But the observer need not worry overmuch about this. He will find that the eye gets so accustomed to it as almost to forget that it is there, so that something of a shock may be experienced when a casual star-gazing friend, on looking at some bright object, remarks, as friends always do, 'What beautiful colours!' Denning records a somewhat extreme case in which a friend, who had been accustomed to observe with a refractor, absolutely resented the absence of the familiar colour fringe in the picture given by a reflector, which is the true achromatic in nature, though not in name. The beginner is recommended to read the article 'The Adjustment of a Small Equatorial,' by Mr. E. W. Maunder, in the *Journal of the British Astronomical Association*, vol. ii., p. 219, where he will find the process of testing described at length and with great clearness.

In making these tests, allowance has, of course, to be made for the state of the atmosphere. A good telescope can only do its best on a good night, and it is not fair to any instrument to condemn it until it has been tested under favourable conditions. The ideal test would be to have its performance tried along with that of another instrument of known good quality and of as nearly the same size as possible. If this cannot be arranged for, the tests must be made on a succession of nights, and good performance on one of these is sufficient to vindicate the reputation of the glass, and to show that any deficiency on other occasions was due to the state of the air, and not to the instrument. Should his telescope pass the above tests satisfactorily, the observer ought to count himself a happy man, and will until he begins to hanker after a bigger instrument.

The mention of the pointing of the telescope to a star brings up the question of how this is to be done. It seems a simple thing; as a matter of fact, with anything like a high magnifying power it is next to impossible; and there are few things more exasperating than to see a star or a planet shining brightly before your eyes, and yet to find yourself quite unable to get it into the field of view. The simple remedy is the addition of a finder to the telescope. This is a small telescope of low magnifying power which is fastened to the larger instrument by means of collars bearing adjusting screws, which enable it to be laid accurately parallel with the large tube (Fig. 10). Its eye-piece is furnished with cross-threads, and a star brought to the intersection of these threads will be in the field of the large telescope. In place of the two threads crossing at right angles there may be substituted three threads interlacing to form a little triangle in the centre of the finder's field. By this device the star can always be seen when the glass is being pointed instead of being hidden, as in the other case, behind the intersection of the two threads. A fine needle-point fixed in the eye-piece will also be found an efficient substitute for the cross-threads. In the absence of a finder the telescope may be pointed by using the lowest power eye-piece and substituting a higher one when the object is in the field; but beyond question the finder is well worth the small addition which it makes to the cost of an instrument. A little care in adjusting the finder now and again will often save trouble and annoyance on a working evening.

The question of a stand on which to mount the telescope now falls to be considered, and is one of great importance, though apt to be rather neglected at first. It will soon be found that little satisfaction or comfort can be had in observing unless the stand adopted is steady. A shaky mounting will spoil the performance of the best telescope that ever was made, and will only tantalize the observer with occasional glimpses of what might be seen under better conditions. Better have a little less aperture to the object-glass, and a good steady mounting, than an extra inch of objective and a mounting which robs you of all comfort in the using of your telescope. Beginners are indeed rather apt to be misled into the idea that the only matters of importance are the objective and its tube, and that money spent on the stand is money wasted. Hence many fearful and wonderful contrivances for doing badly what a little saved in the size of the telescope and expended on the stand would have enabled them to do well. It is very interesting, no doubt, to get a view of Jupiter or Saturn for one field's-breadth, and then to find, on attempting to readjust the instrument for another look, that the mounting has obligingly taken your star-gazing into its own hands, and is now directing your telescope to a different object altogether; but repetition of this form of amusement is apt to pall. A radically weak stand can never be made into a good one; the best plan is to get a properly proportioned mounting at once, and be done with it.

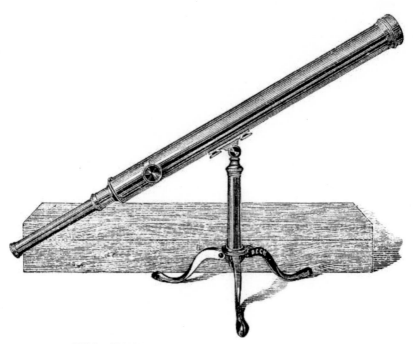

FIG. 9.—SMALL TELESCOPE ON PILLAR AND CLAW STAND.

For small instruments, such as we are dealing with, the mounting generally adopted is that known as the Altazimuth, from its giving two motions, one in altitude and one in azimuth, or, to use more familiar terms, one vertical and the other horizontal. There are various types of the Altazimuth. If the instrument be of not more than 3 feet focal length, the ordinary stand known as the 'pillar and claw' (Fig. 9) will meet all the requirements of this form of motion. Should the focal length be greater than 3 feet, it is advisable to have the instrument mounted on a tripod stand, such as is shown in Fig. 10. In the simpler forms of both these mountings the two motions requisite to follow an object must be given by hand, and it is practically impossible to do this without conveying a certain amount of tremor to the telescope, which disturbs clearness of vision until it subsides, by which time the object to be viewed is generally getting ready to go out of the field again. To obviate this inconvenience as far as possible, the star or planet when found should be placed just outside the field of view, and allowed to enter it by the diurnal motion of the earth. The tremors will thus have time to subside before the object reaches the centre of the field, and this process must be repeated as long as the observation continues. In making this adjustment attention must be paid to the direction of the object's motion through the field, which, of

18

course, varies according to its position in the sky. If it be remembered that a star's motion through the telescopic field is the exact reverse of its true direction across the sky, little difficulty will be found, and use will soon render the matter so familiar that the adjustment will be made almost automatically.

FIG. 10.—TELESCOPE ON TRIPOD, WITH FINDER AND SLOW MOTIONS.

A much more convenient way of imparting the requisite motions is by the employment of tangent screws connected with Hooke's joint-handles, which are brought conveniently near to the hands of the observer as he sits at the eye-end. These screws clamp into circles or portions of circles, which have teeth cut on them to fit the pitch of the screw, and by means of them a slow and steady motion may be imparted to the telescope. When it is required to move the instrument more rapidly, or over a large expanse of sky, the clamps which connect the screws with the circles are slackened, and the motion is given by hand. Fig. 10 shows an instrument provided with these adjuncts, which, though not absolutely necessary, and adding somewhat to the cost of the mounting, are certainly a great addition to the ease and comfort of observation.

FIG. 11.—EQUATORIAL MOUNTING FOR SMALL TELESCOPE.

The Altazimuth mounting, from its simplicity and comparative cheapness, has all along been, and will probably continue to be, the form most used by amateurs. It is, however, decidedly inferior in every respect to the equatorial form of mount. In this form (Fig. 11) the telescope is carried by means of two axes, one of which—the Polar axis—is so adjusted as to be parallel to the pole of the earth's rotation, its degree of inclination being therefore dependent upon the latitude of the place for which it is designed. At the equator it will be horizontal, will lie at an angle of 45 degrees half-way between the equator and either pole, and will be vertical at the poles. At its upper end it carries a cross-head with bearings through which there passes another axis at right angles to the first (the declination axis). Both these axes are free to rotate in their respective bearings, and thus the telescope is capable of two motions, one of which—that of the declination axis—enables the instrument to be set to the elevation of the object to be observed, while the other—that of the polar axis—enables the observer to follow the object, when found, from its rising to its setting by means of a single movement, the telescope sweeping out circles on the sky corresponding to those which the stars themselves describe in their journey across the heavens. This single movement may be given by means of a tangent screw such as has already been described, and the use of a telescope thus equipped is certainly much easier and more convenient than that of an

Altazimuth, where two motions have constantly to be imparted. To gain the full advantage of the equatorial form of mounting, the polar axis must be placed exactly in the North and South line, and unless the mounting can be adjusted properly and left in adjustment, it is robbed of much of its superiority. For large fixed instruments it is, of course, almost universally used; and in observatories the motion in Right Ascension, as it is called, which follows the star across the sky, is communicated to the driving-wheel of the polar axis by means of a clock which turns the rod carrying the tangent screw (Plate II.). These are matters which in most circumstances are outside the sphere of the amateur; it may be interesting for him, however, to see examples of the way in which large instruments are mounted. The frontispiece, accordingly, shows the largest and most perfect instrument at present in existence, while Plate II., with Figs. 4 and 12, give further examples of fine modern work. The student can scarcely fail to be struck by the extreme solidity of the modern mountings, and by the way in which all the mechanical parts of the instrument are so contrived as to give the greatest convenience and ease in working. Comparing, for instance, Plate II., a 6-inch refractor by Messrs. Cooke, of York, available either for visual or photographic work, with the Dorpat refractor (Fig. 3), it is seen that the modern maker uses for a 6-inch telescope a stand much more solid and steady than was deemed sufficient eighty years ago for an instrument of $9\frac{6}{10}$ inches. Attention is particularly directed to the way in which nowadays all the motions are brought to the eye-end so as to be most convenient for the observer, and frequently, as in this case, accomplished by electric power, while the declination circle is read by means of a small telescope so that the large instrument can be directed upon any object with the minimum of trouble. The driving clock, well shown on the right of the supporting pillar, is automatically controlled by electric current from the sidereal clock of the observatory.

**PLATE II.**

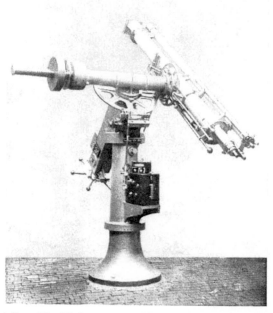

6-inch Photo-Visual Refractor, equatorially mounted. Messrs. T. Cooke & Sons.

We have now to consider the reflecting form of telescope, which, especially in this country, has deservedly gained much favour, and has come to be regarded as in some sense the amateur's particular tool.

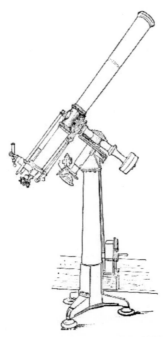

FIG. 12.—8-INCH REFRACTOR ON EQUATORIAL MOUNTING.

As a matter of policy, one can scarcely advise the beginner to make his first essay with a reflector. Its adjustments, though simple enough, are apt to be troublesome at the time when everything has to be learned by experience; and its silver films, though much more durable than is commonly supposed, are easily destroyed by careless or unskilful handling, and require more careful nursing than the objective of a refractor. But, having once paid his first fees to experience, the observer, if he feel so inclined, may venture upon a reflector, which has probably more than sufficient advantages to make up for its weaker points. First and foremost of these advantages stands the not inconsiderable one of cheapness. A 10½-inch reflector may be purchased new for rather less than the sum which will buy a 4-inch refractor. True, the reflector has not the same command of light inch for inch as the refractor, but a reflector of 10½ inches should at least be the match of an 8-inch refractor in this respect, and will be immeasurably more powerful than the 4-inch refractor, which comes nearest to it in price. Second stands the ease and comfort so conspicuous in observing with a Newtonian. Instead of having almost to break his neck craning under the eye-piece of a telescope pointed to near the zenith, the observer with a Newtonian looks always straight in front of him, as the eye-piece of a reflector mounted as an altazimuth is always horizontal, and when the instrument is mounted equatorially, the tube, or its eye-end, is made to rotate so that the line of vision may be kept horizontal. Third is the absence of colour. Colour is not conspicuous in a small refractor, unless the objective be of very bad quality; but as the aperture increases it is apt to become somewhat painfully apparent. The reflector, on the other hand, is truly achromatic, and may be relied upon to show the natural tints of all objects with which it deals. This point is of considerable importance in connection with planetary observation. The colouring of Jupiter, for instance, will be seen in a reflector as a refractor can never show it.

Against these advantages there have to be set certain disadvantages. First, the question of adjustments. A small refractor requires practically none; but a reflector, whatever its size, must be occasionally attended to, or else its mirrors will get out of square and bad performance will be the result. It is easy, however, to make too much of this difficulty. The adjustments of the writer's 8½-inch With reflector have remained for months at a time as perfect as when they had been newly attended to. Second, the renewal of the silver films. This may cause some trouble in the neighbourhood of towns where the atmosphere is such as to tarnish silver quickly; and even in the country a film must be renewed at intervals. But these may be long enough. The film on the mirror above referred to has stood without serious deterioration for five years at a time. Third, the reflector, with its open-mouthed tube, is undoubtedly more subject to disturbance from air currents and changes of temperature, and its mirrors take longer to settle down into good definition after the instrument has been moved from one point of the sky to another. This difficulty cannot be got over, and must be put up with; but it is not very conspicuous with the smaller sizes of telescopes, such as are likely to be in the hands of an amateur at the beginning of his work. There are probably but few nights when an 8½-inch reflector will not give quite a good account of itself in this respect by comparison with a refractor of anything like equal power. On the whole, the state of the question is this: If the observer wishes to have as much power as possible in proportion to his expenditure, and is not afraid to take the risk of a small amount of trouble with the adjustments and films, the reflector is probably the instrument best suited to him. If, on the other hand, he is so situated that his telescope has to be much moved, or, which is almost as bad, has to stand unused for any considerable intervals of time, he will be well advised to prefer a refractor. One further advantage of the reflecting form is that, aperture for aperture, it is very much shorter. The average refractor will probably run to a length of from twelve to fifteen times the diameter of its objective. Reflectors are rarely of a greater length than nine times the diameter of the large mirror, and are frequently shorter still. Consequently, size for size, they can be worked in less space, which is often a consideration of importance.

FIG. 13.—FOUR-FOOT REFLECTOR EQUATORIALLY MOUNTED.

The mountings of the reflector are in principle precisely similar to those of the refractor already described. The greater weight, however, and the convenience of having the body of the instrument kept as low as possible, owing to the fact of the eye-piece being at the upper end of the tube, have necessitated various modifications in the forms to which these principles are applied. Plates III. and IV., and Fig. 13, illustrate the altazimuth and equatorial forms of mounting as applied to reflectors of various sizes, Fig. 13 being a representation of Lassell's great 4-foot reflector.

**PLATE III.**

20-inch Reflector, Stanmore Observatory.

And now, having his telescope, whatever its size, principle, or form of mounting, the observer has to proceed to use it. Generally speaking, there is no great difficulty in arriving at the manner of using either a refractor or a reflector, and for either instrument the details of handling must be learned by experience, as nearly all makers have little variations of their own in the form of clamps and slow motions, though the principles in all instruments are the same. With regard to these, the only recommendation that need be made is one of caution in the use of the glass until its ways of working have been gradually found out. With a knowledge of the principles of its construction and a little application of common-sense, there is no part of a telescope mounting which may not be readily understood. Accordingly, what follows must simply take the form of general hints as to matters which every telescopist ought to know, and which are easier learned once and for all at the beginning than by slow experience. These hints are of course the very commonplaces of observation; but it is the commonplace that is the foundation of good work in everything.

If possible, let the telescope be fixed in the open air. Where money is no object, a few pounds will furnish a convenient little telescope-house, with either a rotating or sliding roof, which enables the instrument to be pointed to any quarter of the heavens. Such houses are now much more easily obtained than they once were, and anyone who has tried both ways can testify how much handier it is to have nothing to do but unlock the little observatory, and find the telescope ready for work, than to have to carry a heavy instrument out into the open. Plate IV. illustrates such a shelter, which has done duty for more than twelve years, covering an 8½-inch With, whose tube and mounting are almost entirely the work of a local smith; and in the *Journal of the British Astronomical Association*, vol. xiv., p. 283, Mr. Edwin Holmes gives a simple description of a small observatory which was put up at a cost of about £3, and has proved efficient and durable. The telescope-house has also the advantage of protecting the observer and his instrument from the wind, so that observation may often be carried on on nights which would be quite too windy for work in the open.

**PLATE IV.**

Telescope House and 8½-inch 'with' Reflector.

Should it not be possible to obtain such a luxury, however, undoubtedly the next best is fairly outside. No one who has garden room should ever think of observing from within doors. If the telescope be used at an open window its definition will be impaired by air-currents. The floor of the room will communicate tremors to the instrument, and every movement of the observer will be accompanied by a corresponding movement of the object in the field, with results that are anything but satisfactory. In some cases no other position is available. If this be so, Webb's advice must be followed, the window opened as widely and as long beforehand as possible, and the telescope thrust out as far as is convenient. But these precautions only palliate the evils of indoor observation. The open air is the best, and with a little care in wrapping up the observer need run no risk.

Provide the telescope, if a refractor, with a dew-cap. Without this precaution dew is certain to gather upon the object-glass, with the result of stopping all observation until it is removed, and the accompanying risk of damage to the objective itself. Some instruments are provided by their makers with dew-caps, and all ought to be; but in the absence of this provision a cap may be easily contrived. A tube of tin three or four times as long as the diameter of the object-glass, made so as to slide fairly stiffly over the object end of the tube where the ordinary cap fits, and blackened inside to a dead black, will remove practically all risk. The blackening may be done with lamp-black mixed with spirit varnish. Some makers—Messrs. Cooke, of York, for instance—line both tube and dew-cap with black velvet. This ought to be ideal, and might be tried in the case of the dew-cap by the observer. Finders are rarely fitted with dew-caps, but certainly should be; the addition will often save trouble and inconvenience.

Be careful to cover up the objective or mirror with its proper cap before removing it into the house. If this is not done, dewing at once results, the very proper punishment for carelessness. This may seem a caution so elementary as scarcely to be worth giving; but it is easier to read and remember a hint than to have to learn by experience, which in the case of a reflector will almost certainly mean a deteriorated mirror film. Should the mirror, if you are using a reflector, become dewed in spite of all precautions, do not attempt to touch the film while it is moist, or you will have the pleasure of seeing it scale off under your touch. Bring it into a room of moderate temperature, or stand it in a through draught of dry air until the moisture evaporates; and should any stain be left, make sure that the mirror is absolutely dry before attempting to polish it off. With regard to this matter of polishing, touch the mirror as seldom as possible with the polishing-pad. Frequent polishing does far more harm than good, and the mirror, if kept carefully covered when not in use, does not need it. A fold of cotton-wool between the cap and the mirror will, if occasionally taken out and dried, help greatly to preserve the film.

Next comes a caution which beginners specially need. Almost everyone on getting his first telescope wants to see everything as big as possible, and consequently uses the highest powers. This is an entire mistake. For a telescope of 2½ inches aperture two eye-pieces, or at most three, are amply sufficient. Of these, one may be low in power, say 25 to 40, to take in large fields, and, if necessary, to serve in place of a finder. Such an eye-piece will give many star pictures of surprising beauty. Another may be of medium power, say 80, for general work; and a third may be as high as 120 for exceptionally fine nights and for work on double stars. Nominally a 2½ inch, if of very fine quality, should bear on the finest nights and on stars a power of 100 to the inch, or 250. Practically it will do nothing of the sort, and on most nights the half of this power will be found rather too high. Indeed, the use of high powers is for many reasons undesirable. A certain proportion of light to size must be preserved in the image, or it will appear faint and 'clothy.' Further, increased magnifying power means also increased magnification of every tremor of the atmosphere; and with high powers the object viewed passes through the field so rapidly that constant shifting of the telescope is required, and only a brief glimpse can be obtained before the instrument has to be moved again. It is infinitely more satisfactory to see your object of a moderate size and steady than to see it much larger, but hazy, tremulous, and in rapid motion. 'In inquiring about the quality of some particular instrument,' remarks Sir Howard Grubb, 'a tyro almost invariably asks, "What is the highest power you can use?" An experienced observer will ask, "What is the lowest power with which you can do so and so?"'

Do not be disappointed if your first views of celestial objects do not come up to your expectations. They seldom do, particularly in respect of the size which the planets present in the field. A good deal of the discouragement so often experienced is due to the idea that the illustrations in text-books represent what ought to be seen by anyone who looks through a telescope. It has to be remembered that these pictures are, for one thing, drawn to a large scale, in order to insure clearness in detail, that they are in general the results of observation with the very finest telescopes, and the work of skilled observers making the most of picked nights. No one would expect to rival a trained craftsman in a first attempt at his trade; yet most people seem to think that they ought to be able at their first essay in telescopic work to see and depict as much as men who have spent half a lifetime in an apprenticeship to the delicate art of observation. Given time, patience, and perseverance, and the skill will come. The finest work shown in good drawings represents, not what the beginner may expect to see at his first view, but a standard towards which he must try to work by steady practice both of eye and hand. In this connection it may be suggested that the observer should take advantage of every opportunity of seeing through larger and finer instruments than his own. This will teach him two things at least. First, to respect his own small telescope, as he sees how bravely it stands up to the larger instrument so far as regards the prominent features of the celestial bodies; and, second, to notice how the superior power of the large glass brings out nothing startlingly different from that which is shown by his own small one, but a wealth of delicate detail which must be looked for (compare Plate XV. with Fig. 22). A little occasional practice with a large instrument will be found a great encouragement and a great help to working with a small one, and most possessors of large glasses are more than willing to assist the owners of small ones.

Do not be ashamed to draw what you see, whether it be little or much, and whether you can draw well or ill. At the worst the result will have an interest to yourself which no representation by another hand can ever possess; at the best your drawings may in course of time come to be of real scientific value. There are few observers who cannot make some shape at a representation of what they see, and steady practice often effects an astonishing improvement. But draw only what you see with certainty. Some observers are gifted with abnormal powers of vision, others with abnormal powers of imagination. Strange to say, the results attained by these two classes differ widely in appearance and in value. You may not be endowed with faculties which will enable you to take rank in the former class; but at least you need not descend to the latter. It is after all a matter of conscience.

Do not be too hasty in supposing that everybody is endowed with a zeal for astronomy equal to your own. The average man or woman does not enjoy being called out from a warm fireside on a winter's night, no matter how beautiful the celestial sight to be seen. Your friend may politely express interest, but to tempt him to this is merely to encourage a habit of untruthfulness. The cause of astronomy is not likely to be furthered by being associated in any person's mind with discomfort and a boredom which is not less real because it is veiled under quite inadequate forms of speech. It is better to wait until the other man's own curiosity suggests a visit to the telescope, if you wish to gain a convert to the science.

When observing in the open be sure to wrap up well. A heavy ulster or its equivalent, and some form of covering for the feet which will keep them warm, are absolute essentials. See that you are thoroughly warm before you go out. In all probability you will be cold enough before work is over; but there is no reason why you should make yourself miserable from the beginning, and so spoil your enjoyment of a fine evening.

Having satisfied his craving for a general survey of everything in the heavens that comes within the range of his glass, the beginner is strongly advised to specialize. This is a big word to apply to the using of a 2½- or 3-inch telescope, but it represents the only way in which interest can be kept up. It does no good, either to the observer or to the science of astronomy, for him to take out his glass, have a glance at Jupiter and another at the Orion nebula, satisfy himself that the two stars of Castor are still two, wander over a few bright clusters, and then turn in, to repeat the same dreary process the next fine night. Let him make up his mind to stick to one, or at most two, objects. Lunar work presents an attractive field for a small instrument, and may be followed on useful lines, as will be pointed out later. A spell of steady work upon Jupiter will at least prepare the way and whet the appetite for a glass more adequate to deal with the great planet. Should star work be preferred, a fine field is opened up in connection with the variable stars, the chief requirement of work in this department being patience and regularity, a small telescope being quite competent to deal with a very large number of interesting objects.

The following comments in Smyth's usual pungent style are worth remembering: 'The furor of a green astronomer is to possess himself of all sorts of instruments—to make observations upon everything—and attempt the determination of quantities which have been again and again determined by competent persons, with better means, and more practical acquaintance with the subject. He starts with an enthusiastic admiration of the science, and the anticipation of new discoveries therein; and all the errors consequent upon the momentary impulses of what Bacon terms "affected dispatch" crowd upon him. Under this course—as soon as the more hacknied objects are "seen up"—and he can decide whether some are greenish-blue or bluish-green—the excitement flags, the study palls, and the zeal evaporates in hyper-criticism on the instruments and their manufacturers.'

This is a true sketch of the natural history, or rather, of the decline and fall, of many an amateur observer. But there is no reason why so ignominious an end should ever overtake any man's pursuit of the study if he will only choose one particular line and make it his own, and be thorough in it. Half-study inevitably ends in weariness and disgust; but the man who will persevere never needs to complain of sameness in any branch of astronomical work.

# CHAPTER III

## THE SUN

From its comparative nearness, its brightness and size, and its supreme importance to ourselves, the sun commands our attention; and in the phenomena which it presents there is found a source of abundant and constantly varying interest. Observation of these phenomena can only be conducted, however, after due precautions have been taken. Few people have any idea of the intense glow of the solar light and heat when concentrated by the object-glass of even a small telescope, and care must be exercised lest irreparable damage be done to the eye. Galileo is said to have finally blinded himself altogether, and Sir William Herschel to have seriously impaired his sight by solar observation. No danger need be feared if one or other of the common precautions be adopted, and some of these will be shortly described; but before we consider these and the means of applying them, let us gather together briefly the main facts about the sun itself.

Our sun, then, is a body of about 866,000 miles in diameter, and situated at a distance of some 92,700,000 miles from us. In bulk it equals 1,300,000 of our world, while it would take about 332,000 earths to weigh it down. Its density, as can be seen from these figures, is very small indeed. Bulk for bulk, it is considerably lighter than the earth; in fact, it is not very much denser than water, and this has very considerable bearing upon our ideas of its constitution.

Natural operations are carried on in this immense globe upon a scale which it is almost impossible for us to realize. A few illustrations gathered from Young's interesting volume, 'The Sun,' may help to make clearer to us the scale of the ruling body of our system. Some conception of the immensity of its distance from us may first be gained from Professor Mendenhall's whimsical illustration. Sensation, according to Helmholtz's experiments, travels at a rate of about 100 feet per second. If, then, an infant were born with an arm long enough to reach to the sun, and if on his birthday he were to exercise this amazing limb by putting his finger upon the solar surface, he would die in blissful ignorance of the fact that he had been burned, for the sensation of burning would take 150 years to travel along that stupendous arm. Were the sun hollowed out like a gigantic indiarubber ball and the earth placed at its centre, the enclosing shell would appear like a far distant sky to us. Our moon would have room to circle within this shell at its present distance of 240,000 miles, and there would still be room for another satellite to move in an orbit exterior to that of the moon at a further distance of more than 190,000 miles. The attractive power of this great body is no less amazing than its bulk. It has been calculated that were the attractive power which keeps our earth coursing in its orbit round the sun to cease, and to be replaced by a material bond consisting of steel wires of a thickness equal to that of the heaviest telegraph-wires, these would require to cover the whole sunward side of our globe in the proportion of nine to each square inch. The force of gravity at the solar surface is such that a man who on the earth weighs 10 stone would, if transported to the sun, weigh nearly 2 tons, and, if he remained of the same strength as on earth, would be crushed by his own weight.

**PLATE V.**

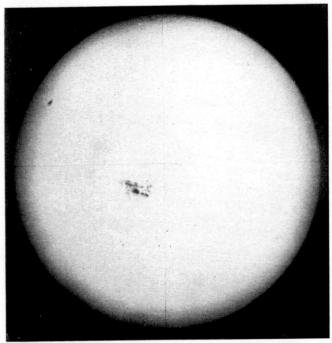

The Sun, February 3, 1905. Royal Observatory, Greenwich.

The first telescopic view of the sun is apt, it must be confessed, to be a disappointment. The moon is certainly a much more attractive subject for a casual glance. Its craters and mountain ranges catch the eye at once, while the solar disc presents an appearance of almost unbroken uniformity. Soon, however, it will become evident that the uniformity is only apparent. Generally speaking, the surface will quickly be seen to be broken up by one or more dark spots (Plate V.), which present an apparently black centre and a sort of grey shading round about this centre. The margin of the disc will be seen to be notably less bright than its central portions; and near the margin, and oftenest, though not invariably, in connection with one of the dark spots, there will be markings of a brilliant white, and often of a fantastically branched shape, which seem elevated above the general surface; while as the eye becomes more used to its work it will be found that even a small telescope brings out a kind of mottled or curdled appearance over the whole disc. This last feature may often be more readily seen by moving the telescope so as to cause the solar image to sweep across the field of view, or by gently tapping the tube so as to cause a slight vibration. Specks of dirt which may have gathered upon the field lens of the eye-piece will also be seen; but these may be distinguished from the spots by moving the telescope a little, when they will shift their place relatively to the other features; and their exhibition may serve to suggest the propriety of keeping eye-pieces as clean as possible.

## PLATE VI.

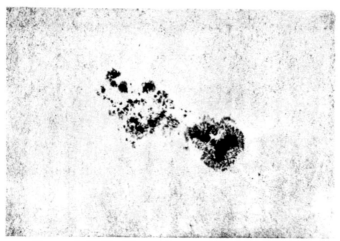

Photograph of Bridged Sunspot (Janssen). *Knowledge*, February, 1890.

The spots when more closely examined will be found to present endless irregularities in outline and size, as will be seen from the accompanying plates and figures. On the whole, there is comparative fidelity to two main features —a dark central nucleus, known as the umbra, and a lighter border, the penumbra; but sometimes there are umbræ which have no penumbra, and sometimes there are spots which can scarcely be called more than penumbral shadings. The shape of the spot is sometimes fairly symmetrical; at other times the most fantastic forms appear. The umbra appears dark upon the bright disc, but is in reality of dazzling lustre, sending to us, according to Langley, 54 per cent. of the amount of heat received from a corresponding area of the brilliant unspotted surface. Within the umbra a yet darker deep, if it be a deep, has been detected by various observers, but is scarcely likely to be seen with the small optical means which we are contemplating. The penumbra is very much lighter in colour than the umbra, and invariably presents a streaked appearance, the lines all running in towards the umbra, and resembling very much the edge of a thatched roof. It will be seen to be very much lighter in colour on the edge next the umbra, while it shades to a much darker tone on that side which is next to the bright undisturbed part of the surface (Figs. 14 and 15). Frequently a spot will be seen interrupted by a bright projection from the luminous surface surrounding it which may even extend from side to side of the spot, forming a bridge across it (Plate VI., and Figs. 16, 17, and 18). These are the outstanding features of the solar spots, and almost any telescope is competent to reveal them. But these appearances have to be interpreted, so far as that is possible, and to have some scale applied to them before their significance can in the least be recognised. The observer will do well to make some attempt at realizing the enormous actual size of the seemingly trifling details which his instrument shows. For example, the spot in Figs. 14 and 15 is identical with that measured by Mr. Denning on the day between the dates of my rough sketches; and its greatest diameter was then 27,143 miles. Spots such as those of 1858, of February, 1892, and February, 1904, have approached or exceeded 140,000 miles in diameter, while others have been frequently recorded, which, though not to be compared to these leviathans, have yet measured from 40,000 to 50,000 miles in diameter, with umbræ of 25,000 to 30,000 miles. Of course, the accurate measurement of the spots demands appliances which are not likely to be in a beginner's hands; but there are various ways of arriving at an approximation which is quite sufficient for the purpose in view—namely, a realization of the scale of any spot as compared with that of the sun or of our own earth.

FIG. 14.—SUN-SPOT, JUNE 18, 1889.

FIG. 15.—SUN-SPOT, JUNE 20, 1889.

Of these methods, the simplest on the whole seems to be that given by Mr. W. F. Denning in his admirable volume, 'Telescopic Work for Starlight Evenings.' Fasten on the diaphragm of an eye-piece (the blackened brass disc with a central hole which lies between the field and eye lenses of the eye-piece) a pair of fine wires at right angles to one another. Bring the edge of the sun up to the vertical wire, the eye-piece being so adjusted that the sun's motion is along the line of the horizontal wire. This can easily be accomplished by turning the eye-piece round until the solar motion follows the line of the wire. Then note the number of seconds which the whole disc of the sun takes to cross the vertical wire. Note, in the second place, the time which the spot to be measured takes to cross the vertical wire; and, having these two numbers, a simple rule of three sum enables the diameter of the spot to be roughly ascertained. For the sun's diameter, 866,000 miles, is known, and the proportion which it bears to the number of seconds which it takes to cross the wire will be the same as that borne by the spot to its time of transit. Thus, to take Mr. Denning's example, if the sun takes 133 seconds to cross the wire, and the spot takes 6·5, then 133 : 866,000 : : 6·5 : 42,323, which latter number will be, roughly speaking, the diameter of the spot in miles. This, method is only a very rough approximation; still, it at least enables the observer to form some conception of the scale of what is being seen. It will answer best when the sun is almost south, and is, of course, less and less accurate as the spot in question is removed from the centre of the disc; for the sun being a sphere, and not a flat surface, foreshortening comes largely and increasingly into play as spots near the edge (or limb) of the disc.

Continued observation will speedily lead to the detection of the exceedingly rapid changes which often affect the spots and their neighbourhood. There are instances in which a spot passes across the disc without any other apparent changes save those which are due to perspective; and the same spot may even accomplish a complete rotation and appear again with but little change. But, generally speaking, it will be noticed that the average spot changes very considerably during the course of a single rotation. Often, indeed, the changes are so rapid as to be apparent within the course of a few hours. Figs. 14 and 15 represent a spot which was seen on June 18 and 20, 1889, and sketched by means of a 2½-inch refractor with a power of 80. A certain proportion of the change noticeable is due to perspective, but there are also changes of considerable importance in the structure of the spot which are actual, and due to motion of its parts. Mr. Denning's drawing ('Telescopic Work,' p. 95) shows the spot on the day between these two representations, and exhibits an intermediate stage of the change. The late Professor Langley has stated that when he was making the exquisite drawing of a typical sun-spot which has become so familiar to all readers of astronomical text-books and periodicals, a portion of the spot equal in area to the continent of South America changed visibly during the time occupied in the execution of the drawing; and this is only one out of many records of similar tenor. Indeed, no one who has paid any attention to solar observation can fail to have had frequent instances of change on a very large scale brought under his notice; and when the reality of such change has been actually witnessed, it brings home to the mind, as no amount of mere statement can, the extraordinary mobility of the solar surface, and the fact that we are here dealing with a body where the conditions are radically different from those with which we are familiar on our own globe. Changes which involve the complete alteration in appearance of areas of many thousand square miles have to be taken into consideration as things of common occurrence upon the sun, and must vitally affect our ideas of his constitution and structure (Figs. 16, 17, 18).

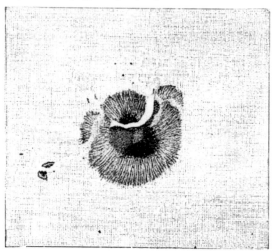

FIG. 16.—SUN-SPOT SEEN IN 1870.

Little more can be done by ordinary observation with regard to the spots and the general surface. Common instruments are not likely to have much chance with the curious structure into which the coarse mottling of the disc breaks up when viewed under favourable circumstances. This structure, compared by Nasmyth to willow-leaves, and by others to rice-grains, is beautifully seen in a number of the photographs taken by Janssen and others; but it is seldom that it can be seen to full advantage.

FIG. 17.—ANOTHER PHASE OF SPOT (FIG. 16).

FIG. 18.—PHASE OF SPOT (FIGS. 16 AND 17).

On the other hand, the spots afford a ready means by which the observer may for himself determine approximately the rotation period of the sun. A spot will generally appear to travel across the solar disc in about 13 days 14½ hours, and to reappear at the eastern limb after a similar lapse of time, thus making the apparent rotation-period 27 days 5 hours. This has to be corrected, as the earth's motion round the sun causes an apparent slackening in the rate of the spots, and a deduction of about 2 days has to be made for this reason, the resulting period being about 25 days 7 hours. It will quickly be found that no single spot can be relied upon to give anything like a precise determination, as many have motions of their own independent of that due to the sun's rotation; and, in addition, there has been shown to be a gradual lengthening of the period in high latitudes. Thus, spots near the equator yield a period of 25·09 days, those in latitude 15° N. or S. one of 25·44, and those in latitude 30° one of 26·53.

This law of increase, first established by Carrington, has been confirmed by the spectroscopic measures of Dunér at Upsala. His periods, while uniformly in excess of those derived from ordinary observations, show the same progression. For 0° his period is 25·46 days, for 15° 26·35, and for 30° 27·57. Continuing his researches up to 15° from the solar pole, Dunér has found that at that point the period of rotation is protracted to 38.5 days.

Reference has already been made to the bright and fantastically branched features which diversify the solar surface, generally appearing in connection with the spots, and best seen near the limb, though existing over the whole disc. These 'faculæ,' as they are called, will be readily seen with a small instrument—I have seen them easily with a 2-inch finder and a power of 30. They suggest at once to the eye the idea that they are elevations above the general surface, and look almost like waves thrown up by the convulsions which produce the spots. The rotation-period given by them has also been ascertained, and the result is shorter than that given by the spots. In latitude 0° it is 24·66 days, at 15° it is 25·26, at 30° 25·48. These varieties of rotation show irresistibly that the sun cannot in any sense of the term be called a rigid body. As Professor Holden remarks: 'It is more like a vast whirlpool, where the velocities of rotation depend on the situation of the rotating masses, not only as to latitude, but also as to depth beneath the rotating surface.' Plate VII., from a photograph of the sun taken by Mr. Hale, in which the surface is portrayed by the light of one single calcium ray of the solar spectrum, presents a view of the mottled appearance of the disc, together with several bright forms which the author of the photograph considers to be faculæ. M. Deslandres, of the Meudon Observatory, who has also been very successful in this new branch of solar photography, considers, however, that these forms are not faculæ, but distinct phenomena, to which he proposes to assign the name 'faculides'; and for various reasons his view appears to be the more probable. They are, however, in any case, in close relation with the faculæ, and, as Miss Clerke observes, 'symptoms of the same disturbance.'

**PLATE VII.**

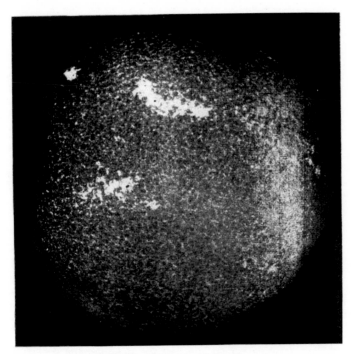

Solar Surface with Faculæ. Yerkes Observatory.

The question of the nature of the sun spots is one that at once suggests itself; but it must be confessed that no very satisfactory answer can yet be given to it. None of the many theories put forward have covered all the observed facts, and an adequate solution seems almost as far off as ever. No one can fail to be struck with the resemblance which the spots present to cavities in the solar surface. Instinctively the mind seems to regard the umbra of the spot as being the centre of a great hollow of which the penumbra represents the sloping sides; and for long it was generally held that Wilson's theory, which assumed this appearance to correspond to an actual fact, was correct. Wilson found by observation of certain spots that when the spot was nearest to one limb the penumbra disappeared, either altogether or in part, on the side towards the centre, and that this process was reversed as the spot approached the opposite limb, the portion of the penumbra nearest the centre of the disc being always the narrowest.

This is the order of appearances which would naturally follow if the spot in question were a cavity; and if it were invariable there could scarcely be any doubt as to its significance. But while the Wilsonian theory has been recognised in all the text-books for many years, there has always been a suspicion that it was by no means adequately established, and that it was too wide an inference from the number of cases observed; and of late years it has been falling more and more into discredit. Howlett, for example, an observer of great experience, has asserted that the appearances on which the theory is based are not the rule, but the exception, and that therefore it must be given up. Numbers of spots seem to present the appearance of elevations rather than of depressions, and altogether it seems as though no category has yet been attained which will embrace all the varieties of spot-form. On this point further observation is very much needed, and the work that has to be done is well within the reach of even moderate instruments.

The fact that sun-spots wax and wane in numbers in a certain definite period was first ascertained by the amateur observer Schwabe of Dessau, whose work is a notable example of what may be accomplished by steadfast devotion to one particular branch of research. Without any great instrumental equipment, Schwabe effected the discovery of this most important fact—a discovery second to none made in the astronomical field during the last century—simply by the patient recording of the state of the sun's face for a period of over thirty years, during which he succeeded in securing an observation, on the average, on about 300 days out of every year. The period now accepted differs slightly from that assigned by him, and amounts to 11·11 years. Beginning with a minimum, when few spots or none may be visible for some time, the spots will be found to increase gradually in number, until, about four and a half years from the minimum, a maximum is reached; and from this point diminution sets in, and results, in about 6·6 years, in a second minimum. The period is not one of absolute regularity—a maximum or a minimum may sometimes lag considerably behind its proper time, owing to causes as yet unexplained. Still, on the whole, the agreement is satisfactory.

This variation is also accompanied by a variation in the latitude of the spots. Generally they follow certain definite zones, mostly lying between 10° and 35° on either side of the solar equator. As a minimum approaches, they tend to appear nearer to the equator than usual; and when the minimum has passed the reappearance of the spots takes the opposite course, beginning in high latitudes.

It has further been ascertained that a close connection exists between the activity which results in the formation of sun-spots, and the electrical phenomena of our earth. Instances of this connection have been so repeatedly observed as to leave no doubt of its reality, though the explanation of it has still to be found. It has been suggested by Young that there may be immediate and direct action in this respect between the sun and the earth, an action perhaps kindred with that solar repulsive force which seems to drive off the material of a comet's tail. As yet not satisfactorily accounted for is the fact that it does not always follow that the appearance of a great sun-spot is answered by a magnetic storm on the earth. On the average the connection is established; but there are many individual instances of sun-spots occurring without any answering magnetic thrill from the earth. To meet this difficulty, Mr. E. W. Maunder has proposed a view of the sun's electrical influence upon our earth, which, whether it be proved or disproved in the future, seems at present the most living attempt to account for the observed facts. Briefly, he considers it indubitably proved—

1. That our magnetic disturbances are connected with the sun.

2. That the sun's action, of whatever nature, is not from the sun as a whole, but from restricted areas.

3. That the sun's action is not radiated, but restricted in direction.

On his view, the great coronal rays or streamers seen in total eclipses (Plate VIII.) are lines of force, and similarly the magnetic influence which the sun exerts upon the earth acts along definite and restricted lines. Thus a disturbance of great magnitude upon the sun would only be followed by a corresponding disturbance on the earth if the latter happened to be at or near the point where it would fall within the sweep of the line of magnetic force emanating from the sun. In proportion as the line of magnetic force approached to falling perpendicularly on the earth, the magnetic disturbance would be large: in proportion as it departed from the perpendicular it would diminish until it vanished finally altogether. The suggestion seems an inviting one, and has at least revived very considerably the interest in these phenomena.

Such, then, are the solar features which offer themselves to direct observation by means of a small telescope. The spots, apart from their own intrinsic interest, are seen to furnish a fairly accurate method by which the observer can determine for himself the sun's rotation period. Their size may be approximately measured, thus conveying to the mind some idea of the enormous magnitude of the convulsions which take place upon this vast globe. The spot zones may be noted, together with the gradual shift in latitude as the period approaches or recedes from minimum; while observations of individual spots may be conducted with a view to gathering evidence which shall help either to confirm or to confute the Wilsonian theory. In this latter department of observation the main requisite is that the work should be done systematically. Irregular observation is of little or no value; but steady work may yield results of high importance. While, however, systematic observation is desirable, it is not everyone who has the time or the opportunity to give this; and to many of us daily solar observation may represent an unattainable ideal. Even if this be the case, there still remains an inexhaustible fund of beauty and interest in the sun-spots. It does not take regular observation to enable one to be interested in the most wonderful intricacy and beauty of the solar detail, in its constant changes, and in the ideas which even casual work cannot fail to suggest as to the nature and mystery of that great orb which is of such infinite importance to ourselves.

A small instrument, used in the infrequent intervals which may be all that can be snatched from the claims of other work, will give the user a far more intelligent interest in the sun, and a far better appreciation of its features, than can be gained by the most careful study of books. In this, and in all other departments of astronomy, there is nothing like a little practical work to give life to the subject.

In the conduct of observation, however, regard must be paid to the caution given at the beginning of this chapter. Various methods have been adopted for minimizing the intense glare and heat. For small telescopes—up to 2½ inches or so—the common device of the interposition of a coloured glass between the eye-piece and the eye will generally be found sufficient on the score of safety, though other arrangements may be found preferable. Such glasses are usually supplied with small instruments, mounted in brass caps which screw or slide on to the ends of the various eye-pieces. Neutral tint is the best, though a combination of green and red also does well. Red transmits too much heat for comfort. Should dark glasses not be supplied, it is easy to make them by smoking a piece of glass to the required depth, protecting it from rubbing by fastening over it a covering glass which rests at each end on a narrow strip of cardboard.

With anything larger than 2½ inches, dark glass is never quite safe. A 3-inch refractor will be found quite capable of cracking and destroying even a fairly thick glass if observation be long continued. The contrivance known as a polarizing eye-piece was formerly pretty much beyond the reach of the average amateur by reason of its costliness. Such eye-pieces are now becoming much cheaper, and certainly afford a most safe and pleasant way of viewing the sun. They are so arranged that the amount of light and heat transmitted can be reduced at will, so as to render the use of a dark glass unnecessary, thus enabling the observer to see all details in their natural colouring. The ordinary solar diagonal, in which the bulk of the rays is rejected, leaving only a small portion to reach the eye, is cheaper and satisfactory, though a light screen-glass is still required with it. But unquestionably the best general method of observing, and also the least costly, is that of projecting the sun's image through the telescope upon a prepared white surface, which may be of paper, or anything else that may be found suitable.

To accomplish this a light framework may be constructed in the shape of a truncated cone. At its narrow end it slips or screws on to the eye-end of the telescope, and it may be made of any length required, in proportion to the size of solar disc which it is desired to obtain. It should be covered with black cloth, and its base may be a board with white paper stretched on it to receive the image, which is viewed through a small door in the side. In place of the board with white paper, other expedients may be tried. Noble recommends a surface of plaster of Paris, smoothed while wet on plate glass, and this is very good if you can get the plaster smooth enough. I have found white paint, laid pretty thickly on glass and then rubbed down to a smooth matt surface by means of cuttle-fish bone, give very satisfactory results. Should it be desired to exhibit the sun's image to several people at once, this can easily be done by projecting it upon a sheet of paper fastened on a drawing-board, and supported at right angles to the telescope by an easel. The framework, or whatever takes its place, being in position, the telescope is pointed at the sun by means of its shadow; when this is perfectly round, or when the shadow of the framework perfectly corresponds to the shape of its larger end, the sun's image should be in the field of view.

# CHAPTER IV

## THE SUN'S SURROUNDINGS

We have now reached the point beyond which mere telescopic power will not carry us, a point as definite for the largest instrument as for the smallest. We have traced what can be seen on the visible sun, but beyond the familiar disc, and invisible at ordinary seasons or with purely telescopic means, there lie several solar features of the utmost interest and beauty, the study of which very considerably modifies our conception of the structure of our system's ruler. These features are only revealed in all their glory and wonder during the fleeting moments in which a total eclipse is central to any particular portion of the earth's surface.

A solar eclipse is caused by the fact that the moon, in her revolution round the earth, comes at certain periods between us and the sun, and obscures the light of the latter body either partially or totally. Owing to the fact that the plane of the orbit in which the moon revolves round the earth does not coincide with that in which the earth revolves round the sun, the eclipse is generally only partial, the moon not occupying the exact line between the centres of the sun and the earth. The dark body of the moon then appears to cut off a certain portion, larger or smaller, of the sun's light; but none of the extraordinary phenomena to be presently described are witnessed. Even during a partial eclipse, however, the observer may find considerable interest in watching the outline of the dark moon, as projected upon the bright background of the sun. It is frequently jagged or serrated, the projections indicating the existence, on the margin of the lunar globe, of lofty mountain ranges.

FIG. 19.—ECLIPSES OF THE SUN AND MOON.

Occasionally the conditions are such that the moon comes centrally between the earth and the sun (Fig. 19), and then an eclipse occurs which may be either total or annular. The proportion between the respective distances from us of the sun and the moon is such that these two bodies, so vastly different in real bulk, are sensibly the same in apparent diameter, so that a very slight modification of the moon's distance is sufficient to reduce her diameter below that of the sun. The lunar orbit is not quite circular, but has a small eccentricity. It may therefore happen that an eclipse occurs when the moon is nearest the earth, at which point she will cover the sun's disc with a little to spare; or the eclipse may occur when she is furthest away from the earth, in which case the lunar diameter will appear less than that of the sun, and the eclipse will be only an annular one, and a bright ring or 'annulus' of sunlight will be seen surrounding the dark body of the moon at the time when the eclipse is central.

All conditions being favourable, however—that is to say, the eclipse being central, and the moon at such a position in her orbit as to present a diameter equal to, or slightly greater than, that of the sun—a picture of extraordinary beauty and wonder reveals itself the moment that totality has been established. The centre of the view is the black disc of the moon. From behind it on every side there streams out a wonderful halo of silvery light which in some of its furthest streamers may sometimes extend to a distance of several million miles. In the Indian Eclipse of 1898, for example, one streamer was photographed by Mrs. Maunder, which extended to nearly six diameters from the limb of the eclipsed sun (Plate VIII.). The structure of this silvery halo is of the most remarkable complexity, and appears to be subject to continual variations, which have already been ascertained to be to some extent periodical and in sympathy with the sun-spot period. At its inner margin this halo rests upon a ring of crimson fire which extends completely round the sun, and throws up here and there great jets or waves, which frequently assume the most fantastic forms and rise to heights varying from 20,000 to 100,000 miles, or in extreme instances to a still greater height. To these appearances astronomers have given the names of the Corona, the Chromosphere, and the Prominences. The halo of silvery light is the Corona, the ring of crimson fire the Chromosphere, and the jets or waves are the Prominences.

**PLATE VIII.**

Coronal Streamers: Eclipse of 1898. From Photographs by Mrs. Maunder.

The Corona is perhaps the most mysterious of all the sun's surroundings. As yet its nature remains undetermined, though the observations which have been made at every eclipse since attention was first directed to it have been gradually suggesting and strengthening the idea that there exists a very close analogy between the coronal streamers and the Aurora or the tails of comets. The extreme rarity of its substance is conclusively proved by the fact that such insubstantial things as comets pass through it apparently unresisted and undelayed. Its structure presents variations in different latitudes. Near the poles it exhibits the appearance of brushes of light, the rays shooting out from the sun towards each summit of his axis, while the equatorial rays curve over, presenting a sort of fish-tail appearance. These variations are modified, as already mentioned, by some cause which is at all events coincident with the sun-spot period. At minimum the corona presents itself with polar brushes of light and fish-tail equatorial rays, the latter being sometimes of the most extraordinary length, as in the case of the eclipse of July 29, 1878, when a pair of these wonderful streamers extended east and west of the eclipsed sun to a distance of at least 10,000,000 miles.

When an eclipse occurs at a spot-maximum, the distribution of the coronal features is found to have entirely changed. Instead of being sharply divided into polar brushes and equatorial wings, the streamers are distributed fairly evenly around the whole solar margin, in a manner suggesting the rays from a star, or a compass-card ornament. The existence of this periodic change has been repeatedly confirmed, and there can be no doubt that the corona reflects in its structure the system of variation which prevails upon the sun. 'The form of the corona,' says M. Deslandres, 'undergoes periodical variations, which follow the simultaneous periodical variations already ascertained for spots, faculæ, prominences, and terrestrial magnetism.' Certainty as to its composition has not yet been attained; nor is this to be wondered at, for the corona is only to be seen in the all too brief moments during which a total eclipse is central, and then only over narrow tracts of country, and all attempts to secure photographs of it at other times have hitherto failed. When examined with the spectroscope, it yields evidence that its light is derived from three sources—from the incandescence of solid or liquid particles, from reflected sunshine, and from gaseous emissions. The characteristic feature of the coronal spectrum is a bright green line belonging to an unknown element which has been named 'coronium.'

The Chromosphere and the Prominences, unlike the elusive corona, may now be studied continuously by means of the spectroscope, and instruments are now made at a comparatively moderate price, which, in conjunction with a small telescope—3 inches will suffice—will enable the observer to secure most interesting and instructive views of both. The chromosphere is, to use Miss Clerke's expression, 'a solar envelope, but not a solar atmosphere.' It surrounds the whole globe of the sun to a depth of probably from 3,000 to 4,000 miles, and has been compared to an ocean of fire, but seems rather to present the appearance of a close bristling covering of flames which rise above the surface of the visible sun like the blades of grass upon a lawn. Any one of these innumerable flames may be elevated into unusual proportions in obedience to the vast and mysterious forces which are at work beneath, and then becomes a prominence. On the whole the constitution of the chromosphere is the same as that of the prominences. Professor Young has found that its normal constituents are hydrogen, helium, coronium, and calcium. But whenever there is any disturbance of its surface, the lines which indicate the presence of these substances are at once reinforced by numbers of metallic lines, indicating the presence of iron, sodium, magnesium, and other substances.

The scale to which these upheavals attain in the prominences is very remarkable. For example, Young records the observation of a prominence on October 7, 1880. When first seen, at about 10.30 a.m., it was about 40,000 miles in height and attracted no special attention. Half an hour later it had doubled its height. During the next hour it continued to soar upwards until it reached the enormous altitude of 350,000 miles, and then broke into filaments which gradually faded away, until by 12.30 there was nothing left of it. On another occasion he recorded one which darted upwards in half an hour from a moderate elevation to a height of 200,000 miles, and in which clouds of hydrogen must have been hurled aloft with a speed of at least 200 miles per second. (Plate IX. gives a representation of the chromosphere and prominences from a photograph by M. Deslandres.) Between the chromosphere and the actual glowing surface of the sun which we see lies what is known as the 'reversing layer,' from the fact that owing to its presence the dark lines of the solar spectrum are reversed in the most beautiful way during the second at the beginning and end of totality in an eclipse. Young, who was the first to observe this phenomenon (December 22, 1870), remarks of it that as soon as the sun has been hidden by the advancing moon, 'through the whole length of the spectrum, in the red, the green, the violet, the bright lines flash out by hundreds and thousands, almost startlingly; as suddenly as stars from a bursting rocket-head, and as evanescent, for the whole thing is over within two or three seconds.'

**PLATE IX.**

The Chromosphere and Prominences, April 11, 1894. Photographed by M. H. Deslandres.

The spectrum of the reversing layer has since been photographed on several occasions—first by Shackleton, at Novaya Zemlya, on August 9, 1896—and its bright lines have been found to be true reversals of the dark lines of the normal solar spectrum. This layer may be described as a thin mantle, perhaps 500 miles deep, of glowing metallic vapours, surrounding the whole body of the sun, and normally, strange to say, in a state of profound quiescence. Its presence was of course an integral part of Kirchhoff's theory of the mode in which the dark lines of the solar spectrum were produced. Such a covering was necessary to stop the rays whose absence makes the dark lines; and it was assumed that the rays so stopped would be seen bright, if only the splendour of the solar light could be cut off. These assumptions have therefore been verified in the most satisfactory manner.

Thus, then, the structure of the sun as now known is very different from the conception of it which would be given by mere naked-eye, or even telescopic, observation. We have first the visible bright surface, or photosphere, with its spots, faculæ, and mottling, and surrounded by a kind of atmosphere which absorbs much of its light, as is evidenced by the fact that the solar limb is much darker than the centre of the disc (Plate V.); next the reversing layer, consisting of an envelope of incandescent vapours, which by their absorption of the solar rays corresponding to themselves give rise to the dark lines in the spectrum. Beyond these again lies the chromosphere, rising into gigantic eruptive or cloud-like forms in the prominences; and yet further out the strange enigmatic corona.

It must be confessed that the reversing layer, the chromosphere, and the corona lie somewhat beyond the bounds and purpose of this volume; but without mention of them any account of the sun is hopelessly incomplete, and it is not at all improbable that a few years may see the spectroscope so brought within the reach of ordinary observers as to enable them in great measure to realize for themselves the facts connected with the complex structure of the sun. In any case, the mere recital of these facts is fitted to convey to the mind a sense of the utter inadequacy of our ordinary conceptions of that great body which governs the motions of our earth, and supplies to it and to the other planets of our system life and heat, light and guidance. With the unaided eye we view the sun as a small tranquil white disc; the telescope reveals to us that it is a vast globe convulsed by storms which involve the upheaval or submersion, within a few hours, of areas far greater than our own world; the spectroscope or the total eclipse adds to this revelation the further conception of a sweltering ocean of flame surrounding the whole solar surface, and rising in great jets of fire which would dissolve our whole earth as a drop of wax is melted in the flame of a candle; while beyond that again the mysterious corona stretches through unknown millions of miles its streamers of silvery light—the great enigma of solar physics. Other bodies in the universe present us with pictures of beautiful symmetry and vast size: some even within our own system suggest by their appearance the presence within their frame of tremendous forces which are still actively moulding them; but the sun gives us the most stupendous demonstration of living force that the mind of man can apprehend. Of course there are many stars which are known to be suns on which processes similar to those we have been considering are being carried on on a yet vaster scale; but the nearness of our sun brings the tremendous energy of these processes home to us in a way that impresses the mind with a sense almost of fear.

'Is it possible,' says Professor Newcomb, 'to convey to the mind any adequate conception of the scale on which natural operations are here carried on? If we call the chromosphere an ocean of fire, we must remember that it is an ocean hotter than the fiercest furnace, and as deep as the Atlantic is broad. If we call its movements hurricanes, we must remember that our hurricanes blow only about 100 miles an hour, while those of the chromosphere blow as far in a single second. They are such hurricanes as, coming down upon us from the north, would, in thirty seconds after they had crossed the St. Lawrence, be in the Gulf of Mexico, carrying with them the whole surface of the continent in a mass not simply of ruin, but of glowing vapour.... When we speak of eruptions, we call to mind Vesuvius burying the surrounding cities in lava; but the solar eruptions, thrown 50,000 miles high, would engulf the whole earth, and dissolve every organized being on its surface in a moment. When the mediæval poets sang, "Dies iræ, dies illa, solvet sæclum in favilla," they gave rein to their wildest imagination without reaching any conception of the magnitude or fierceness of the flames around the sun.'

The subject of the maintenance of the sun's light and heat is one that scarcely falls within our scope, and only a few words can be devoted to it. It is practically impossible for us to attain to any adequate conception of the enormous amount of both which is continually being radiated into space. Our own earth intercepts less than the two thousand millionth part of the solar energy. It has been estimated that if a column of ice 2¼ miles in diameter could be erected to span the huge interval of 92,700,000 miles between the earth and the sun, and if the sun could concentrate the whole of his heat upon it, this gigantic pillar of ice would be dissolved in a single second; in seven more it would be vaporized. The amount of heat developed on each square foot of solar surface is 'equivalent to the continuous evolution of about 10,000 horse-power'; or, as otherwise stated, is equal to that which would be produced by the hourly burning of nine-tenths of a ton of anthracite coal on the same area of 1 square foot.

It is evident, therefore, that mere burning cannot be the source of supply. Lord Kelvin has shown that the sun, if composed of solid coal, would burn itself out in about 6,000 years.

Another source of heat may be sought in the downfall of meteoric bodies upon the solar surface; and it has been calculated that the inrush of all the planets of our system would suffice to maintain the present energy for 45,604 years. But to suppose the existence near the sun of anything like the amount of meteoric matter necessary to account, on this theory, for the annual emission of heat involves consequences which are quite at variance with observed facts, though it is possible, or even practically certain, that a small proportion of the solar energy is derived from this source.

We are therefore driven back upon the source afforded by the slow contraction of the sun. If this contraction happens, as it must, an enormous amount of heat must be developed by the process, so much so that Helmholtz has shown that an annual contraction of 250 feet would account for the total present emission. This contraction is so slow that about 9,500 years would need to elapse before it became measurable with anything like certainty. In the meantime, then, we may assume as a working hypothesis that the light and heat of the central body of our system are maintained, speaking generally, by his steady contraction. Of course this process cannot have gone on, and cannot go on, indefinitely; but as the best authorities have hitherto regarded the date when the sun shall have shrunk so far as to be no longer able to support life on the earth as distant from us by some ten million years, and as the latest investigations on the subject, those of Dr. See, point in the direction of a very large extension of this limit, we may have reasonable comfort in the conviction that the sun will last our time.

# CHAPTER V

## MERCURY

The planet nearest to the sun is not one which has proved itself particularly attractive to observers in the past; and the reasons for its comparative unattractiveness are sufficiently obvious. Owing to the narrow limits of his orbit, he never departs further from the sun either East or West than between 27° and 28°, and the longest period for which he can be seen before sunrise or after sunset is two hours. It follows that, when seen, he is never very far from the horizon, and is therefore enveloped in the denser layers of our atmosphere, and presents the appearance sadly familiar to astronomers under the name of 'boiling,' the outlines of the planet being tremulous and confused. Of course, observers who have powerful instruments provided with graduated circles can find and follow him during the day, and it is in daylight that nearly all the best observations have been secured. But with humbler appliances observation is much restricted; and, in fact, probably many observers have never seen the planet at all.

Views of Mercury, however, such as they are, are by no means so difficult to secure as is sometimes supposed. Denning remarks that he has seen the planet on about sixty-five occasions with the naked eye—that in May, 1876, he saw it on thirteen different evenings, and on ten occasions between April 22 and May 11, 1890; and he states it as his opinion that anyone who will make it a practice to obtain naked-eye views should succeed from about twelve to fifteen times in the year. During the spring of 1905, to take a recent example, Mercury was quite a conspicuous object for some time in the Western sky, close to the horizon, and there was no difficulty whatever in obtaining several views of him both with the telescope and with the naked eye, though the disc was too much disturbed by atmospheric tremors for anything to be made of it telescopically. In his little book, 'Half-hours with the Telescope,' Proctor gives a method of finding the planet which would no doubt prove quite satisfactory in practice, but is somewhat needlessly elaborate. Anyone who takes the pains to note those dates when Mercury is most favourably placed for observation—dates easily ascertained from Whitaker or any other good almanac—and to carefully scan the sky near the horizon after sunset either with the naked eye, or, better, with a good binocular, will scarcely fail to detect the little planet which an old English writer more graphically than gracefully calls 'a squinting lacquey of the sun.'

Mercury is about 3,000 miles in diameter, and circles round the sun at a mean distance of 36,000,000 miles. His orbit is very eccentric, so that when nearest to the sun this distance is reduced to 28,500,000, while when furthest away from him it rises to 43,500,000. The proportion of sunlight which falls upon the planet must therefore vary considerably at different points of his orbit. In fact, when he is nearest to the sun he receives nine times as much light and heat as would be received by an equal area of the earth; but when the conditions are reversed, only four times the same amount. The bulk of the planet is about one-nineteenth that of the earth, but its weight is only one-thirtieth, so that its materials are proportionately less dense than those of our own globe. It is about 3½ times as dense as water, the corresponding figure for the earth being rather more than 5½.

Further, it is apparent that the materials of which Mercury's globe is composed reflect light very feebly. It has been calculated that the planet reflects only 17 per cent. of the light which falls upon it, 83 per cent. being absorbed; and this fact obviously carries with it the conclusion that the atmosphere of this little world cannot be of any great density. For clouds in full sunlight are almost as brilliantly white as new-fallen snow, and if Mercury were surrounded with a heavily cloud-laden atmosphere, he would reflect nearly five times the amount of light which he at present sends out into space.

As his orbit falls entirely within that of our own earth, Mercury, like his neighbour Venus, exhibits phases. When nearest to us the planet is 'new,' when furthest from us it is 'full,' while at the stages intermediate between these points it presents an aspect like that of the moon at its first and third quarters. It may thus be seen going through the complete series from a thin crescent up to a completely rounded disc. The smallness of its apparent diameter, and the poor conditions under which it is generally seen, make the observation of these phases by no means so easy as in the case of Venus; yet a small instrument will show them fairly well. Observers seem generally to agree that the surface has a dull rosy tint, and a few faint markings have, by patient observation, been detected upon it (Fig. 20); but these are far beyond the power of small telescopes. Careful attention to them and to the rate of their apparent motion across the disc has led to the remarkable conclusion that Mercury takes as long to rotate upon his axis as he does to complete his annual revolution in his orbit; in other words, that his day and his year are of the same length—namely, eighty-eight of our days. This conclusion, when announced in 1882 by the well-known Italian observer Schiaparelli, was received with considerable hesitation. It has, however, been confirmed by many observers, notably by Lowell at Flagstaff Observatory, Arizona, and is now generally received, though some eminent astronomers still maintain that really nothing is certainly known as to the period of rotation.

FIG. 20.—MERCURY AS A MORNING STAR. W. F. DENNING, 10-INCH REFLECTOR.

If the long period be accepted, it follows that Mercury must always turn the same face to the sun—that one of his hemispheres must always be scorching under intense heat, and the other held in the grasp of an unrelenting cold of which we can have no conception. 'The effects of these arrangements upon climate,' says Miss Agnes Clerke, 'must be exceedingly peculiar.... Except in a few favoured localities, the existence of liquid water must be impossible in either hemisphere. Mercurian oceans, could they ever have been formed, should long ago have been boiled off from the hot side, and condensed in "thick-ribbed ice" on the cold side.'

From what has been said it will be apparent that Mercury is scarcely so interesting a telescopic object as some of the other planets. Small instruments are practically ruled out of the field by the diminutive size of the disc which has to be dealt with, and the average observer is apt to be somewhat lacking in the patience without which satisfactory observations of an object so elusive cannot be secured. At the same time there is a certain amount of satisfaction and interest in the mere detection of the little sparkling dot of light in the Western sky after the sun has set, or in the Eastern before it has risen; and the revelation of the planet's phase, should the telescope prove competent to accomplish it, gives better demonstration than any diagram can convey of the interior position of this little world. It is consoling to think that even great telescopes have made very little indeed of the surface of Mercury. Schiaparelli detected a number of brownish stripes and streaks, which seemed to him sufficiently permanent to be made the groundwork of a chart, and Lowell has made a remarkable series of observations which reveal a globe seamed and scarred with long narrow markings; but many observers question the reality of these features altogether.

It is perhaps just within the range of possibility that, even with a small instrument, there may be detected that blunting of the South horn of the crescent planet which has been noticed by several reliable observers. But caution should be exercised in concluding that such a phenomenon has been seen, or that, if seen, it has been more than an optical illusion. Those who have viewed Mercury under ordinary conditions of observation will be well aware how extremely difficult it is to affirm positively that any markings on the surface or any deformations of the outline of the disc are real and actual facts, and not due to the atmospheric tremors which affect the little image.

Interesting, though of somewhat rare occurrence, are the transits of Mercury, when the planet comes between us and the sun, and passes as a black circular dot across the bright solar surface. The first occasion on which such a phenomenon was observed was November 7, 1631. The occurrence of this transit was predicted by Kepler four years in advance; and the transit itself was duly observed by Gassendi, though five hours later than Kepler's predicted time. It gives some idea of the uncertainty which attended astronomical calculations in those early days to learn that Gassendi considered it necessary to begin his observations two days in advance of the time fixed by Kepler. If, however, the time of a transit can now be predicted with almost absolute accuracy, it need not be forgotten that this result is largely due to the labours of men who, like Kepler, by patient effort and with most imperfect means, laid the foundations of the most accurate of all sciences.

The next transit of Mercury available for observation will take place on November 14, 1907. It may be noted that during transits certain curious appearances have been observed. The planet, for example, instead of appearing as a black circular dot, has been seen surrounded with a luminous halo, and marked by a bright spot upon its dark surface. No satisfactory explanation of these appearances has been offered, and they are now regarded as being of the nature of optical illusions, caused by defects in the instruments employed, or by fatigue of the eye. It might, however, be worth the while of any who have the opportunity of observing the transit of 1907 to take notice whether these features do or do not present themselves. For their convenience it may be noted that the transit will begin about eleven o'clock on the forenoon of November 14, and end about 12.45.

# CHAPTER VI

## VENUS

Next in order to Mercury, proceeding outwards from the sun, comes the planet Venus, the twin-sister, so to speak, of the earth, and familiar more or less to everybody as the Morning and Evening Star. The diameter of Venus, according to Barnard's measures with the 36-inch telescope of the Lick Observatory, is 7,826 miles; she is therefore a little smaller than our own world. Her distance from the sun is a trifle more than 67,000,000 miles, and her orbit, in strong contrast with that of Mercury, departs very slightly from the circular. Her density is a little less than that of the earth.

There is no doubt that, to the unaided eye, Venus is by far the most beautiful of all the planets, and that none of the fixed stars can for a moment vie with her in brilliancy. In this respect she is handicapped by her position as an inferior planet, for she never travels further away from the sun than 48°, and, even under the most favourable circumstances, cannot be seen for much more than four hours after sunset. Thus we never have the opportunity of seeing her, as Mars and Jupiter can be seen, high in the South at midnight, and far above the mists of the horizon. Were it possible to see her under such conditions, she would indeed be a most glorious object. Even as it is, with all the disadvantages of a comparatively low position and a denser stratum of atmosphere, her brilliancy is extremely striking, having been estimated, when at its greatest, at about nine times that of Sirius, which is the brightest of all the fixed stars, and five times that of Jupiter when the giant planet is seen to the best advantage. It is, in fact, so great that, when approaching its maximum, the shadows cast by the planet's light are readily seen, more especially if the object casting the shadow have a sharply defined edge, and the shadow be received upon a white surface—of snow, for instance. This extreme brilliance points to the fact that the surface of Venus reflects a very large proportion of the sunlight which falls upon it—a proportion estimated as being at least 65 per cent., or not very much less than that reflected by newly fallen snow. Such reflective power at once suggests an atmosphere very dense and heavily cloud-laden; and other observations point in the same direction. So that in the very first two planets of the system we are at once confronted with that diversity in details which coexists throughout with a broad general likeness as to figure, shape of orbit, and other matters. Mercury's reflective power is very small, that of Venus is exceedingly great; Mercury's atmosphere seems to be very attenuated, that of Venus, to all appearance, is much denser than that of our own earth.

Periodically, when Venus appears in all her splendour in the Western sky, one meets with the suggestion that we are having a re-appearance of the Star of Bethlehem; and it seems to be a perpetual puzzle to some people to understand how the same body can be both the Morning and the Evening Star. Those who have paid even the smallest attention to the starry heavens are not, however, in the least likely to make any mistake about the sparkling silver radiance of Venus; and it would seem as though the smallest application of common-sense to the question of the apparent motion of a body travelling round an almost circular orbit which is viewed practically edgewise would solve for ever the question of the planet's alternate appearance on either side of the sun. Such an orbit must appear practically as a straight line, with the sun at its middle point, and along this line the planet will appear to travel like a bead on a wire, appearing now on one side of the sun, now on another. If the reader will draw for himself a diagram of a circle (sufficiently accurate in the circumstances), with the sun in the centre, and divide it into two halves by a line supposed to pass from his eye through the sun, he will see at once that when this circle is viewed edgewise, and so becomes a straight line, a planet travelling round it is bound to appear to move back and forward along one half of it, and then to repeat the same movement along the other half, passing the sun in the process.

Like Mercury, and for the same reason of a position interior to our orbit, Venus exhibits phases to us, appearing as a fully illuminated disc when she is furthest from the earth, as a half-moon at the two intermediate points of her orbit, and as a new moon when she is nearest to us. The actual proof of the existence of these phases was one of the first-fruits which Galileo gathered by means of his newly invented telescope. It is said that Copernicus predicted their discovery, and they certainly formed one of the conclusive proofs of the correctness of his theory of the celestial system. It was the somewhat childish custom of the day for men of science to put forth the statement of their discoveries in the form of an anagram, over which their fellow-workers might rack their brains; probably this was done somewhat for the same reason which nowadays makes an inventor take out a patent, lest someone should rob the discoverer of the credit of his discovery before he might find it convenient to make it definitely public. Galileo's anagram, somewhat more poetically conceived than the barbarous alphabetic jumble in which Huygens announced his discovery of the nature of Saturn's ring, read as follows: 'Hæc immatura a me jam frustra leguntur o. y.' This, when transposed into its proper order, conveyed in poetic form the substance of the discovery: 'Cynthiæ figuras æmulatur Mater Amorum' (The Mother of the Loves [Venus] imitates the phases of Cynthia). It is true that two letters hang over the end of the original sentence, but too much is not to be expected of an anagram.

As a telescopic object, Venus is apt to be a little disappointing. Not that her main features are difficult to see, or are not beautiful. A 2-inch telescope will reveal her phases with the greatest ease, and there are few more exquisite sights than that presented by the silvery crescent as she approaches inferior conjunction. It is a picture which in its way is quite unique, and always attractive even to the most hardened telescopist.

Still, what the observer wants is not merely confirmation of the statement that Venus exhibits phases. The physical features of a planet are always the most interesting, and here Venus disappoints. That very brilliant lustre which makes her so beautiful an object to the naked eye, and which is even so exquisite in the telescopic view, is a bar to any great progress in the detection of the planet's actual features. For it means that what we are seeing is not really the surface of Venus, but only the sunward side of a dense atmosphere —the 'silver lining' of heavy clouds which interpose between us and the true surface of the planet, and render it highly improbable that anything like satisfactory knowledge of her features will ever be attained. Newcomb, indeed, roundly asserts that all markings hitherto seen have been only temporary clouds and not genuine surface markings at all; though this seems a somewhat absolute verdict in view of the number of skilled observers who have specially studied the planet and assert the objective reality of the markings they have detected. The blunting of the South horn of the planet, visible in Mr. MacEwen's fine drawing (Plate X.), is a feature which has been noted by so many observers that its reality must be conceded. On the other hand, some of the earlier observations recording considerable irregularities of the terminator (margin of the planet between light and darkness), and detached points of light at one of the horns, must seemingly be given up. Denning, one of the most careful of observers, gives the following opinion: 'There is strong negative evidence among modern observations as to the existence of abnormal features, so that the presence of very elevated mountains must be regarded as extremely doubtful.... The detached point at the South horn shown in Schröter's telescope was probably a false appearance due to atmospheric disturbances or instrumental defects.' It will be seen, therefore, that the observer should be very cautious in inferring the actual existence of any abnormal features which may be shown by a small telescope; and the more remarkable the features shown, the more sceptical he may reasonably be as to their reality. The chances are somewhat heavily in favour of their disappearance under more favourable conditions of seeing.

**PLATE X.**

Venus. H. MacEwen. 5-inch Refractor.

The same remark applies, with some modifications, to the dark markings which have been detected on the planet by all sorts of observers with all sorts of telescopes. There is no doubt that faint grey markings, such as those shown in Plate X., are to be seen; the observations of many skilled observers put this beyond all question. Even Denning, who says that personally he has sometimes regarded the very existence of these markings as doubtful, admits that 'the evidence affirming their reality is too weighty and too numerously attested to allow them to be set aside'; and Barnard, observing with the Lick telescope, says that he has repeatedly seen markings, but always so 'vague and ill-defined that nothing definite could be made of them.'

The observations of Lowell and Douglass at Flagstaff, Arizona, record quite a different class of markings, consisting of straight, dark, well-defined lines; as yet, however, confirmation of these remarkable features is scanty, and it will be well for the beginner who, with a small telescope and in ordinary conditions of observing, imagines he has detected such markings to be rather more than less doubtful about their reality. The faint grey areas, which are real features, at least of the atmospheric envelope, if not of the actual surface, are beyond the reach of small instruments. Mr. MacEwen's drawings, which accompany this chapter, were made with a 5-inch Wray refractor, and represent very well the extreme delicacy of these markings. I have suspected their existence when observing with an 8½-inch With reflector in good air, but could never satisfy myself that they were really seen.

Up till the year 1890 the rotation period of Venus was usually stated at twenty-three hours twenty-one minutes, or thereby, though this figure was only accepted with some hesitation, as in order to arrive at it there had to be some gentle squeezing of inconvenient observations. But in that year Schiaparelli announced that his observations were only consistent with a long period of rotation, which could not be less than six months, and was not greater than nine. The announcement naturally excited much discussion. Schiaparelli's views were strongly controverted, and for a time the astronomical world seemed to be almost equally divided in opinion. Gradually, however, the conclusion has come to be more and more accepted that Venus, like Mercury, rotates upon her axis in the same time as she takes to make her journey round the sun—in other words, that her day and her year are of the same length, amounting to about 225 of our days. In 1900 the controversy was to some extent reopened by the statement of the Russian astronomer Bélopolsky that his spectroscopic investigations pointed to a much more rapid rotation—to a period, indeed, considerably shorter than twenty-four hours. It is difficult, however, to reconcile this with the absence of polar flattening in the globe of Venus. Lowell's spectroscopic observations are stated by him to point to a period in accordance with his telescopic results —namely, 225 days. The matter can scarcely be regarded as settled in the meantime, but the balance of evidence seems in favour of the longer period.

Another curious and unexplained feature in connection with the planet is what is frequently termed the 'phosphorescence' of the dark side. This is an appearance precisely similar to that seen in the case of the moon, and known as 'the old moon in the young moon's arms.' The rest of the disc appears within the bright crescent, shining with a dull rusty light. In the case of Venus, however, an explanation is not so easily arrived at as in that of the moon, where, of course, earth-light accounts for the visibility of the dark portion. Had the planet been possessed of a satellite, the explanation might have lain there; but Venus has no moon, and therefore no moonlight to brighten her unilluminated portion; and our world is too far distant for earth-shine to afford an explanation. It has been suggested that electrical discharges similar to the aurora may be at the bottom of the mystery; but this seems a little far-fetched, as does also the attribution of the phenomenon to real phosphorescence of the oceans of Venus. Professor Newcomb cuts the Gordian knot by observing: 'It is more likely due to an optical illusion.... To whatever we might attribute the light, it ought to be seen far better after the end of twilight in the evening than during the daytime. The fact that it is not seen then seems to be conclusive against its reality.' But the appearance cannot be disposed of quite so easily as this, for it is not accurate to say that it is only seen in the daytime, and against Professor Newcomb's dictum may be set the judgment of the great majority of the observers who have made a special study of the planet.

We may, however, safely assign to the limbo of exploded ideas that of the existence of a satellite of Venus. For long this object was one of the most persistent of astronomical ghosts, and refused to be laid. Observations of a companion to the planet, much smaller, and exhibiting a similar phase, were frequent during the eighteenth century; but no such object has presented itself to the far finer instruments of modern times, and it may be concluded that the moon of Venus has no real existence.

Venus, like Mercury, transits the sun's disc, but at much longer intervals which render her transits among the rarest of astronomical events. Formerly they were also among the most important, as they were believed to furnish the most reliable means for determining the sun's distance; and most of the estimates of that quantity, up to within the last twenty-five years, were based on transit of Venus observations. Now, however, other methods, more reliable and more readily applicable, are coming into use, and the transit has lost somewhat of its former importance. The interest and beauty of the spectacle still remain; but it is a spectacle not likely to be seen by any reader of these pages, for the next transit of Venus will not take place until June, 2004.

As already indicated, Venus presents few opportunities for useful observation to the amateur. The best time for observing, as in the case of Mercury, is in broad daylight; and for this, unless in exceptional circumstances, graduated circles and a fairly powerful telescope are required. Practically the most that can be done by the possessor of a small instrument is to convince himself of the reality of the phases, and of the non-existence of a satellite of any size, and to enjoy the exquisite and varying beauty of the spectacle which the planet presents. Should his telescope be one of the small instruments which show hard and definite markings on the surface, he may also consider that he has learned a useful lesson as to the possibility of optical illusion, and, incidentally, that he may be well advised to procure a better glass when the opportunity of doing so presents itself. The 'phosphorescence' of the dark side may be looked for, and it may be noted whether it is not seen after dark, or whether it persists and grows stronger. Generally speaking, observations should be made as early in the evening as the planet can be seen in order that the light of the sky may diminish as much as possible the glare which is so evident when Venus is viewed against a dark background.

# CHAPTER VII

## THE MOON

Our attention is next engaged by the body which is our nearest neighbour in space and our most faithful attendant and useful servant. The moon is an orb of 2,163 miles in diameter, which revolves round our earth in a slightly elliptical orbit, at a mean distance of about 240,000 miles. The face which she turns to us is a trifle greater in area than the Russian Empire, while her total surface is almost exactly equal to the areas of North and South America, islands excluded. Her volume is about $2/99$ of that of the earth; her materials are, however, much less dense than those of which our world is composed, so that it would take about eighty-one moons to balance the earth. One result of these relations is that the force of gravity at the lunar surface is only about one-sixth of that at the surface of the earth, so that a twelve-stone man, if transported to the moon, would weigh only two stone, and would be capable of gigantic feats in the way of leaping and lifting weights. The fact of the diminished force of gravity is of importance in the consideration of the question of lunar surfacing.

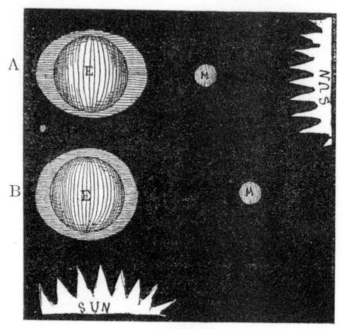

FIG. 21.—THE TIDES.

A, Spring Tide (New Moon); B, Neap Tide.

The most conspicuous service which our satellite performs for us is that of raising the tides. The complete statement of the manner in which she does this would be too long for our pages; but the general outline of it will be seen from the accompanying rough diagram (Fig. 21), which, it must be remembered, makes no attempt at representing the scale either of the bodies concerned or of their distances from one another, but simply pictures their relations to one another at the times of spring and neap tides. The moon (M in Fig. 21, A) attracts the whole earth towards it. Its attraction is greatest at the point nearest to it, and therefore the water on the moonward side is drawn up, as it were, into a heap, making high tide on that side of the earth. But there is also high tide at the opposite side, the reason being that the solid body of the earth, which is nearer to the moon than the water on the further side, is more strongly attracted, and so leaves the water behind it. Thus there are high tides at the two opposite sides of the earth which lie in a straight line with the moon, and corresponding low tides at the intermediate positions. Tides are also produced by the attraction of the sun, but his vastly greater distance causes his tide-producing power to be much less than that of the moon. His influence is seen in the difference between spring and neap tides. Spring tides occur at new or full moon (Fig. 21, A, case of new moon). At these two periods the sun, moon, and earth, are all in one straight line, and the pull of the sun is therefore added to that of the moon to produce a spring tide. At the first and third quarters the sun and moon are at right angles to one another; their respective pulls therefore, to some extent, neutralize each other, and in consequence we have neap tide at these seasons.

**PLATE XI.**

The Moon, April 5, 1900. Paris Observatory.

No one can fail to notice the beautiful set of phases through which the moon passes every month. A little after the almanac has announced 'new moon,' she begins to appear as a thin crescent low down in the West, and setting shortly after the sun. Night by night we can watch her moving eastward among the stars, and showing more and more of her illuminated surface, until at first quarter half of her disc is bright. The reader must distinguish this real eastward movement from the apparent east to west movement due to the daily rotation of the earth. Its reality can readily be seen by noting the position of the moon relatively to any bright star. It will be observed that if she is a little west of the star on one night, she will have moved to a position a little east of it by the next. Still moving farther East, she reaches full, and is opposite to the sun, rising when he sets, and setting when he rises. After full, her light begins to wane, till at third quarter the opposite half of her disc is bright, and she is seen high in the heavens in the early morning, a pale ghost of her evening glories. Gradually she draws nearer to the sun, thinning down to the crescent shape again until she is lost once more in his radiance, only to re-emerge and begin again the same cycle of change.

The time which the moon actually takes to complete her journey round the earth is twenty-seven days, seven hours, and forty-three minutes; and if the earth were fixed in space, this period, which is called the *sidereal month*, would be the actual time from new moon to new moon. While the moon has been making her revolution, however, the earth has also been moving onwards in its journey round the sun, so that the moon has a little further to travel in order to reach the 'new moon' position again, and the time between two new moons amounts to twenty-nine days, twelve hours, forty-four minutes. This period is called a *lunar month*, and is also the *synodic period* of our satellite, a term which signifies generally the period occupied by any planet or satellite in getting back to the same position with respect to the sun, as observed from the earth.

The fact that the moon shows phases signifies that she shines only by reflected light; and it is surprising to notice how little of the light that falls upon her is really reflected by her. On an ordinarily clear night most people would probably say that the moon is much brighter than any terrestrial object viewed in the daytime, when it also is lit by the sun, as the moon is. Yet a very simple comparison will show that this is not so. If the moon be compared during the daytime with the clouds floating around her, she will be seen to be certainly not brighter than they, generally much less bright; indeed, even an ordinary surface of sandstone will look as bright as her disc. In fact, the reason of her great apparent brightness at night is merely the contrast between her and the dark background against which she is seen; a fragment of our own world, put in her place, would shine quite as brightly, perhaps even more so. It is possibly rather difficult at first to realize that our earth is shining to the moon and to the other planets as they do to us, but anyone who watches the moon for a few days after new will find convincing evidence of the fact. Within the arms of the thin crescent can be seen the whole body of the lunar globe, shining with a dingy coppery kind of light—'the ashen light,' as it is called. People talk of this as 'the old moon in the young moon's arms,' and weather-wise (or foolish) individuals pronounce it to be a sign of bad weather. It is, of course, nothing of the sort, for it can be seen every month when the sky is reasonably clear; but it is the sign that our world shines to the other worlds of space as they do to her; for this dim light upon the part of the moon unlit by the sun is simply the light which our own world reflects from her surface to the moon. In amount it is thirteen times more than that which the moon gives to us, as the earth presents to her satellite a disc thirteen times as large as that exhibited by the latter.

The moon's function in causing eclipses of the sun has already been briefly alluded to. In turn she is herself eclipsed, by passing behind the earth and into the long cone of shadow which our world casts behind it into space (Fig. 19). It is obvious that such eclipses can only happen when the moon is full. A total eclipse of the moon, though by no means so important as a solar eclipse, is yet a very interesting and beautiful sight. The faint shadow or penumbra is often scarcely perceptible as the moon passes through it; but the passage of the dark umbra over the various lunar formations can be readily traced, and is most impressive. Cases of 'black eclipses' have been sometimes recorded, in which the moon at totality has seemed actually to disappear as though blotted out of the heavens; but in general this is not the case. The lunar disc still remains visible, shining with a dull coppery light, something like the ashen light, but of a redder tone. This is due to the fact that our earth is not, like its satellite, a next to airless globe, but is possessed of a pretty extensive atmosphere. By this atmosphere those rays of the sun which would otherwise have just passed the edge of the world are caught and refracted so that they are directed upon the face of the eclipsed moon, lighting it up feebly. The redness of the light is due to that same atmospheric absorption of the green and blue rays which causes the body of the setting sun to seem red when viewed through the dense layer of vapours near the horizon. When the moon appears totally eclipsed to us, the sun must appear totally eclipsed to an observer stationed on the moon. A total solar eclipse seen from the moon must present features of interest differing to some extent from those which the similar phenomenon exhibits to us. The duration of totality will be much longer, and, in addition to the usual display of prominences and corona, there will be the strange and weird effect of the black globe of our world becoming gradually bordered with a rim of ruddy light as our atmosphere catches and bends the solar rays inwards upon the lunar surface.

In nine cases out of ten the moon will be the first object to which the beginner turns his telescope, and he will find in our satellite a never-failing source of interest, and a sphere in which, by patient observation and the practice of steadily recording what is seen, he may not only amuse and instruct himself, but actually do work that may become genuinely useful in the furtherance of the science. The possession of powerful instrumental means is not an absolute essential here, for the comparative nearness of the object brings it well within the reach of moderate glasses. The writer well remembers the keen feeling of delight with which he first discovered that a very humble and commonplace telescope—nothing more, in fact, than a small ordinary spy-glass with an object-glass of about 1 inch in aperture—was able to reveal many of the more prominent features of lunar scenery; and the possessor of any telescope, no matter whether its powers be great or small, may be assured that there is enough work awaiting him on the moon to occupy the spare time of many years with one of the most enthralling of studies. The view that is given by even the smallest instrument is one of infinite variety and beauty; and its interest is accentuated by the fact that the moon is a sphere where practically every detail is new and strange.

If the moon be crescent, or near one or other of her quarters at the time of observation, the eye will at once be caught by a multitude of circular, or nearly circular depressions, more clearly marked the nearer they are to the line of division between the illuminated and unilluminated portions of the disc. (This line is known as the Terminator, the circular outline, fully illuminated, being called the Limb). The margins of some of these depressions will be seen actually to project like rings of light into the darkness, while their interiors are filled with black shadow (Plates XI., XIII., XV., and XVI.). At one or two points long bright ridges will be seen, extending for many miles across the surface, and marking the line of one or other of the prominent ranges of lunar mountains (Plates XI., XIII., XVI., XVII.); while the whole disc is mottled over with patches of varied colour, ranging from dark grey up to a brilliant yellow which, in some instances, nearly approaches to white.

If observation be conducted at or near the full, the conditions will be found to have entirely changed. There are now very few ruggednesses visible on the edge of the disc, which now presents an almost smooth circular outline, nor are there any shadows traceable on the surface. The circular depressions, formerly so conspicuous, have now almost entirely vanished, though the positions and outlines of a few of them may still be traced by their contrast in colour with the surrounding regions. The observer's attention is now claimed by the extraordinary brilliance and variety of the tones which diversify the sphere, and particularly by the curious systems of bright streaks radiating from certain well-marked centres, one of which, the system originating near Tycho, a prominent crater not very far from the South Pole, is so conspicuous as to give the full moon very much the appearance of a badly-peeled orange (Plate XII.).

**PLATE XII.**

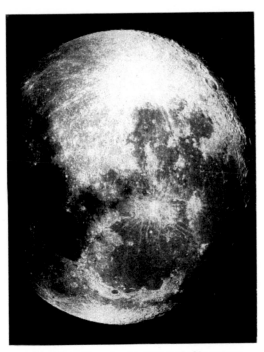

The Moon, November 13, 1902. Paris Observatory.

As soon as the moon has passed the full, the ruggedness of its margin begins once more to become apparent, but this time on the opposite side; and the observer, if he have the patience to work late at night or early in the morning, has the opportunity of seeing again all the features which he saw on the waxing moon, but this time with the shadows thrown the reverse way—under evening instead of under morning illumination. In fact the character of any formation cannot be truly appreciated until it has been carefully studied under the setting as well as under the rising and meridian sun.

We must now turn our attention to the various types of formation which are to be found upon the moon. These may be roughly summarized as follows: (1) The great grey plains, commonly known as Maria, or seas; (2) the circular or approximately circular formations, known generally as the lunar craters, but divided by astronomers into a number of classes to which reference will be made later; (3) the mountain ranges, corresponding with more or less closeness to similar features on our own globe; (4) the clefts or rills; (5) the systems of bright rays, to which allusion has already been made.

1. THE GREAT GREY PLAINS.—These are, of course, the most conspicuous features of the lunar surface. A number of them can be easily seen with the

naked eye; and, so viewed, they unite with the brighter portions to form that resemblance to a human face—'the man in the moon'—with which everyone is familiar. A field-glass or small telescope brings out their boundaries with distinctness, and suggests a likeness to our own terrestrial oceans and seas. Hence the name Maria, which was applied to them by the earlier astronomers, whose telescopes were not of sufficient power to reveal more than their broader outlines. But a comparatively small aperture is sufficient to dispel the idea that these plains have any right to the title of 'seas.' The smoothness which at first suggests water proves to be only relative. They are smooth compared with the brighter regions of the moon, which are rugged beyond all terrestrial precedent; but they would probably be considered no smoother than the average of our own non-mountainous land surfaces. A 2 or 2½-inch telescope will reveal the fact that they are dotted over with numerous irregularities, some of them very considerable. It is indeed not common to find a crater of the largest size associated with them; but, at the same time, craters which on our earth would be considered huge are by no means uncommon upon their surface, and every increase of telescopic power reveals a corresponding increase in the number of these objects (Plates XIII., XV., XVII.).

### PLATE XIII.

The Moon, September 12, 1903. Paris Observatory.

Further, the grey plains are characterized by features of which instances may be seen with a very small instrument, though the more delicate specimens require considerable power—namely, the long winding ridges which either run concentrically with the margins of the plains, or cross their surface from side to side. Of these the most notable is the great serpentine ridge which traverses the Mare Serenitatis in the north-west quadrant of the moon. As it runs, approximately, in a north and south direction, it is well placed for observation, and even a low power will bring out a good deal of remarkable detail in connection with it. It rises in some places to a height of 700 or 800 feet (Neison), and is well shown on many of the fine lunar photographs now so common. Another point of interest in connection with the Maria is the existence on their borders of a number of large crater formations which present the appearance of having had their walls breached and ruined on the side next the mare by the action of some obscure agency. From consideration of these ruined craters, and of the 'ghost craters,' not uncommon on the plains, which present merely a faint outline, as though almost entirely submerged, it has been suggested, by Elger and others, that the Maria, as we see them represent, not the beds of ancient seas, but the consolidated crust of some fluid or viscous substance such as lava, which has welled forth from vents connected with the interior of the moon, overflowing many of the smaller formations, and partially destroying the walls of these larger craters. Notable instances of these half-ruined formations will be found in Fracastorius (Plate XIX., No. 78, and Plate XI.), and Pitatus (Plate XIX., No. 63, and Plate XV.). The grey plains vary in size from the vast Oceanus Procellarum, nearly 2,000,000 square miles in area, down to the Mare Humboldtianum, whose area of 42,000 square miles is less than that of England.

2. The Circular, or Approximately Circular Formations.—These, the great distinguishing feature of lunar scenery, have been classified according to the characteristics, more or less marked, which distinguish them from one another, as walled-plains, mountain-rings, ring-plains, craters, crater-cones, craterlets, crater-pits, and depressions. For general purposes we may content ourselves with the single title craters, using the more specific titles in outstanding instances.

**PLATE XIV.**

Region of Maginus: Overlapping Craters. Paris Observatory.

To these strange formations we have scarcely the faintest analogy on earth. Their multitude will at once strike even the most casual observer. Galileo compared them to the 'eyes' in a peacock's tail, and the comparison is not inapt, especially when the moon is viewed with a small telescope and low powers. In the Southern Hemisphere particularly, they simply swarm to such an extent that the district near the terminator presents much the appearance of a honeycomb with very irregular cells, or a piece of very porous pumice (Plate XIV.). Their vast size is not less remarkable than their number. One of the most conspicuous, for example, is the great walled-plain Ptolemäus, which is well-placed for observation near the centre of the visible hemisphere. It measures 115 miles from side to side of its great rampart, which, in at least one peak, towers more than 9,000 feet above the floor of the plain within. The area of this enormous enclosure is about equal to the combined areas of Yorkshire, Lancashire, and Westmorland—an extent so vast that an observer stationed at its centre would see no trace of the mountain-wall which bounds it, save at one point towards the West, where the upper part of the great 9,000-feet peak already referred to would break the line of the horizon (Plate XIX., No. 111; Plate XIII.).

Nor is Ptolemäus by any means the largest of these objects. Clavius, lying towards the South Pole, measures no less than 142 miles from wall to wall, and includes within its tremendous rampart an area of at least 16,000 square miles. The great wall which encloses this space, itself no mean range of mountains, stands some 12,000 feet above the surface of the plain within, while in one peak it rises to a height of 17,000 feet. Clavius is remarkable also for the number of smaller craters associated with it. There are two conspicuous ones, one on the north, one on the south side of its wall, each about twenty-five miles in diameter, while the floor is broken by a chain of four large craters and a considerable number of smaller ones.

Though unfavourably placed for observation, there is no lunar feature which can compare in grandeur with Clavius when viewed either at sunrise or sunset. At sunrise the great plain appears first as a huge bay of black shadow, so large as distinctly to blunt the southern horn of the moon to the naked eye. As the sun climbs higher, a few bright points appear within this bay of darkness—the summits of the walls of the larger craters—these bright islands gradually forming fine rings of light in the shadow which still covers the floor of the great plain. In the East some star-like points mark where the peaks of the eastern wall are beginning to catch the dawn. Then delicate streaks of light begin to stream across the floor, and the dark mass of shadow divides itself into long pointed shafts, which stretch across the plain like the spires of some great cathedral. The whole spectacle is so magnificent and strange that no words can do justice to it; and once seen it will not readily be forgotten. Even a small telescope will enable the student to detect and draw the more important features of this great formation; and for those whose instruments are more powerful there is practically no limit to the work that may be done on Clavius, which has never been studied with the minuteness that so great and interesting an object deserves. (Clavius is No. 13, Plate XIX. See also Plates XIII. and XV., and Fig. 22, the latter a rough sketch with a 2⅝-inch refractor.)

From such gigantic forms as these, the craters range downwards in an unbroken sequence through striking objects such as Tycho and the grand Copernicus, both distinguished for their systems of bright rays, as well as for their massive and regular ramparts, to tiny pits of black shadow, a few hundred feet across, and with no visible walls, which tax the powers of the very finest instruments. Schmidt's great map lays down nearly 33,000 craters, and it is quite certain that these are not nearly all which can be seen even with a moderate-sized telescope.

**PLATE XV.**

Clavius, Tycho, and Mare Nubium. Yerkes Observatory.

As to the cause which has resulted in this multitude of circular forms, there is no definite consensus of opinion. Volcanic action is the agency generally invoked; but, even allowing for the diminished force of gravity upon the moon, it is difficult to conceive of volcanic action of such intensity as to have produced some of the great walled-plains. Indeed, Neison remarks that such formations are much more akin to the smaller Maria, and bear but little resemblance to true products of volcanic action. But it seems difficult to tell where a division is to be made, with any pretence to accuracy, between such forms as might certainly be thus produced and those next above them in size. The various classes of formation shade one into the other by almost imperceptible degrees.

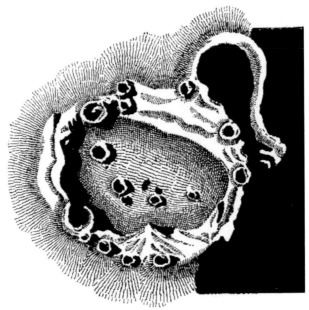

FIG. 22.

CLAVIUS, June 7, 1889, 10 p.m., 2⅝ inch.

3. THE MOUNTAIN RANGES.—These are comparatively few in number, and are never of such magnitude as to put them, like the craters, beyond terrestrial standards of comparison. The most conspicuous range is that known as the Lunar Apennines, which runs in a north-west and south-east direction for a distance of upwards of 400 miles along the border of the Mare Imbrium, from which its mass rises in a steep escarpment, towering in one instance (Mount Huygens) to a height of more than 18,000 feet. On the western side the range slopes gradually away in a gentle declivity. The spectacle presented by the Apennines about first quarter is one of indescribable grandeur. The shadows of the great peaks are cast for many miles over the surface of the Mare Imbrium, magnificently contrasting with the wild tract of hill-country behind, in which rugged summits and winding valleys are mingled in a scene of confusion which baffles all attempt at delineation. Two other important ranges

—the Caucasus and the Alps—lie in close proximity to the Apennines; the latter of the two notable for the curious Alpine Valley which runs through it in a straight line for upwards of eighty miles. This wonderful chasm varies in breadth from about two miles, at its narrowest neck, to about six at its widest point. It is closely bordered, for a considerable portion of its length, by almost vertical cliffs thousands of feet in height, and under low magnifying powers appears so regular as to suggest nothing so much as the mark of a gigantic chisel, driven by main force through the midst of the mountain mass. The Alpine Valley is an easy object, and a power of 50 on a 2-inch telescope will show its main outlines quite clearly. Indeed, the whole neighbourhood is one which will well repay the student, some of the finest of the lunar craters, such as Plato, Archimedes, Autolycus, and Aristillus, lying in the immediate vicinity (Plates XIII. and XVII.).

### PLATE XVI.

Region of Theophilus and Altai Mountains. Yerkes Observatory.

Among the other mountain-ranges may be mentioned the Altai Mountains, in the south-west quadrant (Plate XVI.), the Carpathians, close to the great crater Copernicus, and the beautiful semicircle of hills which borders the Sinus Iridum, or Bay of Rainbows, to the east of the Alpine range. This bay forms one of the loveliest of lunar landscapes, and under certain conditions of illumination its eastern cape, the Heraclides Promontory, presents a curious resemblance, which I have only seen once or twice, to the head of a girl with long floating hair—'the moon-maiden.' The Leibnitz and Doerfel Mountains, with other ranges whose summits appear on the edge of the moon, are seldom to be seen to great advantage, though they are sometimes very noticeably projected upon the bright disc of the sun during the progress of an eclipse.[*] They embrace some of the loftiest lunar peaks reaching 26,000 feet in one of or two instances, according to Schröter and Mädler.

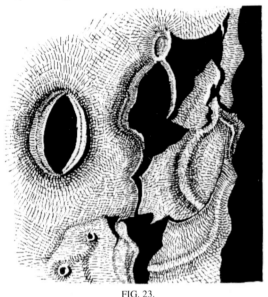

FIG. 23.

ARISTARCHUS and HERODOTUS, February 20, 1891, 6.15 p.m., 3⅞ inch.

4. THE CLEFTS OR RILLS.—In these, and in the ray-systems, we again meet with features to which a terrestrial parallel is absolutely lacking. Schröter of Lilienthal was the first observer to detect the existence of these strange chasms, and since his time the number known has been constantly increasing, till at present it runs to upwards of a thousand. These objects range from comparatively coarse features, such as the Herodotus Valley (Fig. 23), and the well-known Ariadæus and Hyginus clefts, down to the most delicate threads, only to be seen under very favourable conditions, and taxing the powers of the finest instruments. They present all the appearance of cracks in a shrinking surface, and this is the explanation of their existence which at present seems to find most favour. In some cases, such as that of the great Sirsalis cleft, they extend to a length of 300 miles; their breadth varies from

half a mile, or less, to two miles; their depth is very variously estimated, Nasmyth putting it at ten miles, while Elger only allows 100 to 400 yards. In a number of instances they appear either to originate from a small crater, or to pass through one or more craters in their course. The student will quickly find out for himself that they frequently affect the neighbourhood of one or other of the mountain ranges (as, for example, under the eastern face of the Apennines, Plate XVII.), or of some great crater, such as Archimedes. They are also frequently found traversing the floor of a great walled-plain, and at least forty have been detected in the interior of Gassendi (Plate XIX., No. 90). Smaller instruments are, of course, incompetent to reveal more than a few of the larger and coarser of these strange features. The Serpentine Valley of Herodotus, the cleft crossing the floor of Petavius, and the Ariadæus and Hyginus rills are among the most conspicuous, and may all be seen with a 2½-inch telescope and a power of 100.

**PLATE XVII.**

Apennines, Alps, and Caucasus. Paris Observatory.

5. THE SYSTEMS OF BRIGHT RAYS, radiating from certain craters, remain the most enigmatic of the features of lunar scenery. Many of these systems have been traced and mapped, but we need only mention the three principal—those

connected with Tycho, Copernicus, and Kepler, all shown on Plate XII. The Tycho system is by far the most noteworthy, and at once attracts the eye when even the smallest telescope is directed towards the full moon. The rays, which are of great brilliancy, appear to start, not exactly from the crater itself, but from a greyish area surrounding it, and they radiate in all directions over the surface, passing over, and almost completely masking in their course some of the largest of the lunar craters. Clavius, for example, and Maginus (Plate XIV.), become at full almost unidentifiable from this cause, though Neison's statement that 'not the slightest trace of these great walled-plains, with their extremely lofty and massive walls, can be detected in full,' is certainly exaggerated. The rays are not well seen save under a high sun—*i.e.*, at or near full, though some of them can still be faintly traced under oblique illumination.

In ordinary telescopes, and to most eyes, the Tycho rays appear to run on uninterruptedly for enormous distances, one of them traversing almost the whole breadth of the moon in a north-westerly direction, and crossing the Mare Serenitatis, on whose dark background it is conspicuous. Professor W. H. Pickering, who has made a special study of the subject under very favourable conditions, maintains, however, that this appearance of great length is an illusion, and that the Tycho rays proper extend only for a short distance, being reinforced at intervals by fresh rays issuing from small craters on their track. The whole subject is one which requires careful study with the best optical means.

None of the other ray-systems are at all comparable with that of Tycho, though those in connection with Copernicus and Kepler are very striking. As to the origin and nature of these strange features, little is known. There are almost as many theories as there are systems; but it cannot be said that any particular view has commanded anything like general acceptance. Nasmyth's well-known theory was that they represented cracks in the lunar surface, caused by internal pressure, through which lava had welled forth and spread to a considerable distance on either side of the original chasm. Pickering suggests that they may be caused by a deposit of white powder, pumice, perhaps, emitted by the craters from which the rays originate. Both ideas are ingenious, but both present grave difficulties, and neither has commended itself to any very great extent to observers, a remark which applies to all other attempts at explanation.

Such are the main objects of interest upon the visible hemisphere of our satellite. In observing them, the beginner will do well, after the inevitable preliminary debauch of moon-gazing, during which he may be permitted to range over the whole surface and observe anything and everything, not to attempt an attack on too wide a field. Let him rather confine his energies to the detailed study of one or two particular formations, and to the delineation of all their features within reach of his instrument under all aspects and illuminations. By so doing he will learn more of the actual condition of the lunar surface than by any amount of general and haphazard observation; and may, indeed, render valuable service to the study of the moon.

Neither let him think that observations made with a small telescope are now of no account, in view of the number of large instruments employed, and of the great photographic atlases which are at present being constructed. It has to be remembered that the famous map of Beer and Mädler was the result of observations made with a 3¾-inch telescope, and that Lohrmann used an instrument of only 4⅘ inches, and sometimes one of 3¼. Anyone who has seen the maps of these observers will not fail to have a profound respect for the work that can be done with very moderate means. Nor have even the beautiful photographs of the Paris, Lick, and Yerkes Observatories superseded as yet the work of the human eye and hand. The best of the Yerkes photographs, taken with a 40-inch refractor, are said to show detail 'sufficiently minute to tax the powers of a 6-inch telescope.' But this can be said only of a very few photographs; and, generally speaking, a good 3-inch glass will show more detail than can be seen on any but a few exceptionally good negatives.

In conducting his observations, the student should be careful to outline his drawing on such a scale as will permit of the easy inclusion of all the details which he can see, otherwise the sketch will speedily become so crowded as to be indistinct and valueless. A scale of 1 inch to about 20 miles, corresponding roughly to 100 inches to the moon's diameter, will be found none too large in the case of formations where much detail has to be inserted—that is to say, in the case of the vast majority of lunar objects. Further, only such a moderate amount of surface should be selected for representation as can be carefully and accurately sketched in a period of not much over an hour at most; for, though the lunar day is so much longer than our own, yet the changes in aspect of the various formations due to the increasing or diminishing height of the sun become very apparent if observation be prolonged unduly; and thus different portions of the sketch represent different angles of illumination, and the finished drawing, though true in each separate detail, will be untrue as a whole.

Above all, care must be taken to set down only what is seen with certainty, *and nothing more.* The drawing may be good or bad, but it must be true. A coarse or clumsy sketch which is truthful to the facts seen is worth fifty beautiful works of art where the artist has employed imagination or recollection to eke out the meagre results of observation. The astronomer's primary object is to record facts, not to make pictures. If he is skilful in recording what he sees, his sketch will be so much the more truthful; but the facts must come first. Such practical falsehoods as the insertion of uncertain details, or the practice of drawing upon one's recollection of the work of other observers, or of altering portions of a sketch which do not please the eye, are to be studiously avoided. The observer's record of what he has seen should be above suspicion. It may be imperfect; it should never be false. Such cautions may seem superfluous, but a small acquaintance with the subject of astronomical drawing will show that they are not.

The want of a good lunar chart will speedily make itself felt. Fortunately in these days it can be easily supplied. The great photographic atlases now appearing are, of course, for the luxurious; and the elaborate maps of Beer and Mädler or Schmidt are equally out of the question for beginners. The smaller chart of the former observers is, however, inexpensive and good, though a little crowded. For a start there is still nothing much better than Webb's reduction of Beer and Mädler's large chart, published in 'Celestial Objects for Common Telescopes.' It can also be obtained separately; but requires to be backed before use. Mellor's chart is also useful, and is published in a handy form, mounted on mill-board. Those who wish charts between these and the more elaborate ones will find their wants met by such books as those of Neison or Elger. Neison's volume contains a chart in twenty-two sections on a scale of 2 feet to the moon's diameter. It includes a great amount of detail, and is accompanied by an elaborate description of all the features delineated. Its chief drawbacks are the fact that it was published thirty years ago, and that it is an extremely awkward and clumsy volume to handle, especially in the dim light of an observatory. Elger's volume is, perhaps, for English students, the handiest general guide to the moon. Its chart is on a scale of 18 inches to the moon's diameter, and is accompanied by a full description. With either this or Webb's chart, the beginner will find himself amply provided with material for many a long and delightful evenings work.

**PLATE XVIII.**

Chart of the Moon. Nasmyth and Carpenter.

**PLATE XIX.**

Key to Chart of Moon. Nasmyth and Carpenter.

The small chart which accompanies this chapter, and which, with its key-map, I owe to the courtesy of Mr. John Murray, the publisher of Messrs. Nasmyth and Carpenter's volume on the moon, is not in any sense meant as a substitute for those already mentioned, but merely as an introduction to some of the more prominent features of lunar scenery. The list of 229 named and numbered formations will be sufficient to occupy the student for some time; and the essential particulars with regard to a few of the more important formations are added in as brief a form as possible (Appendix I.).

Before we leave our satellite, something must be said as to the conditions prevailing on her surface. The early astronomers who devoted attention to lunar study were drawn on in their labours largely by the hope of detecting resemblances to our own earth, or even traces of human habitation. Schröter and Gruithuisen imagined that they had discovered not only indications of a lunar atmosphere, but also evidence of change upon the surface, and traces of the handiwork of lunarian inhabitants. Gruithuisen, in particular, was confident that in due time it would become possible to trace the cities and the works of the Lunarians. Gradually these hopes have receded into the distance. The existence of a lunar atmosphere is, indeed, no longer positively denied now, as it was a few years ago; but it is certain that such atmosphere as may exist is of extreme rarity, quite inadequate to support animal life as we understand such a thing. Certain delicate changes of colour which take place within some of the craters—Plato for instance—have been referred to vegetation; and Professor Pickering has intimated his observation of something which he considers to be the forming and melting of hoar-frost within certain areas, Messier and a small crater near Herodotus among others. But the observations at best are very delicate and the inferences uncertain. It cannot be denied that the moon may have an atmosphere; but positive traces of its existence are so faint that, even if their reality be admitted, very little can be built upon them.

At the same time when the affirmation is made that the moon is 'a world where there is no weather, and where nothing ever happens,' the most careful modern students of lunar matters would be the first to question such a statement. Even supposing it to be true that no concrete evidence of change upon the lunar surface can be had, this would not necessarily mean that no change takes place. The moon has certainly never been studied to advantage with any power exceeding 1,000, and the average powers employed have been much less. Nasmyth puts 300 as about the profitable limit, and 500 would be almost an outside estimate for anything like regular work. But even assuming the use of a power of 1,000, that means that the moon is seen as large as though she were only 240 miles distant from us. The reader can judge how entirely all but the very largest features of our world would be lost to sight at such a distance, and how changes involving the destruction of large areas might take place and the observer be none the wiser. When it is remembered that even at this long range we are viewing our object through a sea of troubled air of which every tremor is magnified in proportion to the telescopic power employed, until the finer details are necessarily blurred and indistinct, it will be seen that the case has been understated. Indeed it may be questioned if the moon has ever been as well seen as though it had been situated at a distance of 500 miles from the earth. At such a distance nothing short of the vastest cataclysms would be visible; and it is therefore going quite beyond the mark to assume that nothing ever happens on the moon simply because we do not see it happening. Moreover, the balance of evidence does appear to be inclining, slightly perhaps, but still almost unquestionably, towards the view that change does occur upon the moon. Some of the observations which seem to imply change may be explained on other grounds; but there is a certain residuum which appears to defy explanation, and it is very noteworthy that while those who at once dismiss the idea of lunar change are, generally speaking, those who have made no special study of the moon's surface, the contrary opinion is most strongly maintained by eminent observers who have devoted much time to our satellite with the best modern instruments to aid them in their work.

The admission of the possibility of change does not, however, imply anything like fitness for human habitation. The moon, to use Beer and Mädler's oft-quoted phrase, is 'no copy of the earth'; and the conditions of her surface differ widely from anything that we are acquainted with. The extreme rarity of her atmosphere must render her, were other conditions equally favourable, an ideal situation for an observatory. From her surface the stars, which are hidden from us in the daytime by the diffused light in our air, would be visible at broad noonday; while multitudes of the smaller magnitudes which here require telescopic power would there be plain to the unaided eye. The lunar night would be lit by our own earth, a gigantic moon, presenting a surface more than thirteen times as large as that which the full moon offers us, and hanging almost stationary in the heavens, while exhibiting all the effects of rapid rotation upon its own axis. Those appendages of the sun, which only the spectroscope or the fleeting total eclipse can reveal to us, the corona, the chromosphere, and the prominences, would there be constantly visible.

Our astronomers who are painfully wrestling with atmospheric disturbance, and are gradually being driven from the plains to the summits of higher and higher hills in search of suitable sites for the giant telescopes of to-day, may well long for a world where atmospheric disturbance must be unknown, or at least a negligible quantity.

* See drawings by Colonel Markwick with 2¾-inch refractor, of the eclipse of August 30, 1905, 'The Total Solar Eclipse, 1905,' British Astronomical Association, pp. 59, 60.

# CHAPTER VIII

## MARS

The Red Planet is our nearest neighbour on the further, as Venus is on the hither side. He is also in some ways the planet best situated for our observation; for while the greatest apparent diameter of his disc is considerably less than that of Venus, he does not hide close to the sun's rays like the inferior planets, but may be seen all night when in opposition.* Not all oppositions, however, are equally favourable. Under the best circumstances he may come as near to us as 35,000,000 miles; when less favourably situated, he may come no nearer than 61,000,000. This very considerable variation in his distance arises from the eccentricity of the planet's orbit, which amounts to nearly one-tenth, and, so far as we are concerned, it means that his disc is three times larger when he comes to opposition at his least distance from the sun than it is when the conditions are reversed. Under the most favourable circumstances—*i.e.*, when opposition and perihelion† occur together, he presents, it has been calculated, a disc of the same diameter as a half sovereign held up 2,000 yards from the spectator. Periods of opposition recur at intervals of about 780 days, and at the more favourable ones the planet's brilliancy is very striking. The 1877 opposition was very notable in this respect, and in others connected with the study of Mars, and that which preceded the Crimean War was also marked by great brilliancy. Readers of Tennyson will remember how Maud

'Seem'd to divide in a dream from a band of the blest,

And spoke of a hope for the world in the coming wars—

... and pointed to Mars

As he glow'd like a ruddy shield on the Lion's breast.'

Ancient records tell us of his brightness having been so great on some occasions as to create a panic. Panics were evidently more easily created by celestial phenomena then than they are now; but possibly such statements have to be taken with a small grain of salt.

The diameter of Mars is 4,200 miles. In volume he is equal to one-seventh of the world; but his density is somewhat smaller, so that nine globes such as Mars would be required to balance the earth. He turns upon his axis in twenty-four hours thirty-seven minutes, and as the inclination of the axis is not much different from that of our own world he will experience seasonal effects somewhat similar to the changes of our own seasons. The Martian seasons, however, will be considerably longer than ours, as the year of Mars occupies 687 days, and they will be further modified by the large variation which his distance from the sun undergoes in the course of his year—the difference between his greatest and least distances being no less than 26,500,000 miles.

The telescopic view of Mars at once reveals features of considerable interest. We are no longer presented with anything like the beautiful phases of Venus, though Mars does show a slight phase when his position makes a right angle with the sun and the earth. This phase, however, never amounts to more than a dull gibbosity, like that of the moon two or three days before or after full— the most uninteresting of phases. But the other details which are visible much more than atone for any deficiency in this respect. The brilliant ruddy star expands under telescopic power into a broad disc whose ground tint is a warm ochre. This tint is diversified in two ways. At the poles there are brilliant patches of white, larger or smaller according to the Martian season; while the whole surface of the remaining orange-tinted portion is broken up by patches and lines of a dark greenish-grey tone. The analogy with Arctic and Antarctic ice and snow-fields, and with terrestrial continents and seas, is at once and almost irresistibly suggested, although, as will be seen, there are strong reasons for not pressing it too far.

The dark markings, though by no means so sharply defined as the outlines of lunar objects, are yet evidently permanent features; at least this may be confidently affirmed of the more prominent among them. Some of these can be readily recognised on drawings dating from 200 years back, and have served to determine with very satisfactory accuracy the planet's rotation period. In accordance with the almost irresistible evidence which the telescope was held to present, these features were assumed to be seas, straits and bays, while the general ochre-tinted portion of the planet's surface was considered to be dry land. On this supposition the land area of Mars amounts to $5/7$ of the planet's surface, water being confined to the remaining $2/7$. But it is by no means to be taken as an accepted fact that the dark and light areas do represent water and land. One fact most embarrassing to those who hold this traditional view is that in the great wealth of detail which observation with the huge telescopes of to-day has accumulated the bulk belongs to the dark areas. Gradations of shade are seen constantly in them; delicate details are far more commonly to be observed upon them than upon the bright portions of the surface, and several of the 'canals' have been traced clear through the so-called seas. Speaking of his observations of Mars in 1894 with the 36-inch refractor of the Lick observatory, Professor Barnard says: 'Though much detail was shown on the bright "continental" regions, the greater amount was visible on the so-called "seas."… During these observations the impression seemed to force itself upon me that I was actually looking down from a great altitude upon just such a surface as that in which our observatory was placed. At these times there was no suggestion that the view was one of far-away seas and oceans, but exactly the reverse.' Such observations are somewhat disconcerting to the old belief, which, nevertheless, continues to maintain itself, though in somewhat modified form.

It is indeed difficult, if not impossible, to explain the observed facts with regard, for instance, to the white polar caps, on any other supposition than that of the existence of at least a considerable amount of water upon the planet. These caps are observed to be large after the Martian winter has passed over each particular hemisphere. As the season progresses, the polar cap diminishes, and has even been seen to melt away altogether. In one of the fine drawings by the Rev. T. E. R. Phillips, which illustrate this chapter (Plate XX.), the north polar snow will be seen accompanied by a dark circular line, concerning which the author of the sketch says: 'The *melting* cap is always girdled by a narrow and intensely dark line. This is not seen when the cap is forming.' It is hard to believe that this is anything else than the result of the melting of polar snows, and where there is melting snow there must be water. Such results as those obtained by Professor Pickering by photography point in the same direction. In one of his photographs the polar cap was shown much shrunken; in another, taken a few days later, it had very considerably increased in dimensions—as one would naturally conclude, from a fall of snow in the interval. The quantity of water may not be anything like so great as was at one time imagined; still, to give any evidence of its presence at all at a distance of 40,000,000 miles it must be very considerable, and must play an important part in the economy of the planet.

**PLATE XX.**

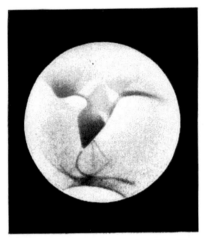
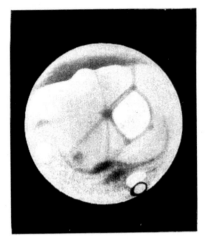

Mars: Drawing 1, January 30, 1899—12 hours.
hours.

$\lambda = 301°, \varphi = +10°.$

Drawing 2, April 22, 1903—10

$\lambda = 200°, \varphi = +24°.$

Rev. T. E. R. Phillips.

In 1877 Schiaparelli of Milan announced that he had discovered that the surface of Mars was covered with a network of lines running with perfect straightness often for hundreds of miles across the surface, and invariably connecting two of the dark areas. To these markings he gave the name of 'canali,' a word which has been responsible for a good deal of misunderstanding. Translated into our language by 'canals,' it suggested the work of intelligent beings, and imagination was allowed to run riot over the idea of a globe peopled by Martians of superhuman intelligence and vast engineering skill. The title 'canals' is still retained; but it should be noted that the term is not meant to imply artificial construction any more than the term 'rill' on the moon implies the presence of water.

At the next opposition of Mars, Schiaparelli not only rediscovered his canals, but made the astonishing announcement that many of them were double, a second streak running exactly parallel to the first at some distance from it. His observations were received with a considerable amount of doubt and hesitation. Skilled observers declared that they could see nothing in the heavens the least corresponding to the network of hard lines which the Italian observer drew across the globe of Mars; and therein to some extent they were right, for the canals are not seen with that hardness of definition with which they are sometimes represented. But, at the same time, each successive opposition has added fresh proof of the fact that Schiaparelli was essentially right in his statement of what was seen. The question of the doubling of the canals is still under dispute, and it seems probable that it is not a real objective fact existing upon the planet, but is merely an optical effect due to contrast. There can be no question, however, about the positive reality of a great number of the canals themselves; their existence is too well attested by observers of the highest skill and experience. 'There is really no doubt whatever,' says Mr. Denning, 'about the streaked or striated configuration of the Northern hemisphere of Mars. The canals do not appear as narrow straight deep lines in my telescope, but as soft streams of dusky material with frequent condensations.' The drawings by Mr. Phillips well represent the surface of the planet as seen with an instrument of considerable power; and the reader will notice that his representation of the canals agrees remarkably well with Denning's description. The 'soft streams with frequent condensations' are particularly well shown on the drawing of April 22, 1903, which represents the region of 200° longitude (see Chart, Plate XXI.) on the centre of the disc. 'The main results of Professor Schiaparelli's work,' remarks Mr. Phillips, 'are imperishable and beyond question. During recent years some observers have given to the so-called "canals" a hardness and an artificiality which they do not possess, with the result that discredit has been brought upon the whole canal system.... But of the substantial accuracy and truthfulness (as a basis on which to work) of the planet's configuration as charted by the great Italian in 1877 and subsequent years, there is in my mind no doubt.' The question of the reality of the canal system may almost be said to have received a definite answer from the remarkable photographs of Mars secured in May, 1905, by Mr. Lampland at the Flagstaff Observatory, which prove that, whatever may be the nature of the canals, the principal ones at all events are actual features of the planet's surface.

Much attention has been directed within the last few years to the observations of Lowell, made with a fine 24-inch refractor at the same observatory, which is situated at an elevation of over 7,000 feet. His conclusion as to the reality of the canals is most positive; but in addition to his confirmation of their existence, he has put forward other views with regard to Mars which as yet have found comparatively few supporters. He has pointed out that in almost all instances the canals radiate from certain round spots which dot the surface of the planet. These spots, which have been seen to a certain extent by other observers, he calls 'oases,' using the term in its ordinary terrestrial significance. His conclusions are, briefly, as follows: That Mars has an atmosphere; that the dark regions are not seas, but marshy tracts of vegetation; that the polar caps are snow and ice, and the reddish portions of the surface desert land. The canals he holds to be waterways, lined on either bank by vegetation, so that we see, not the actual canal, but the green strip of fertilized land through which it passes, while the round dark spots or 'oases' he believes to be the actual population centres of the planet, where the inhabitants cluster to profit by the fertility created by the canals. In support of this view he adduces the observed fact that the canals and oases begin to darken as the polar caps melt, and reasons that this implies that the water set free by the melting of the polar snows is conveyed by artificial means to make the wilderness rejoice.

Lowell's theories may seem, very likely are, somewhat fanciful. It must be remembered, however, that the ground facts of his argument are at least unquestionable, whatever may be thought of his inferences. The melting of the polar caps is matter of direct observation; nor can it be questioned that it is followed by the darkening of the canal system. It is probably wiser not to dogmatize upon the reasons and purposes of these phenomena, for the very sufficient reason that we have no means of arriving at any certitude. Terrestrial analogies cannot safely be used in connection with a globe whose conditions are so different from those of our own earth. The matter is well summed up by Miss Agnes Clerke: 'Evidently the relations of solid and liquid in that remote orb are abnormal; they cannot be completely explained by terrestrial analogies. Yet a series of well-authenticated phenomena are intelligible only on the supposition that Mars is, in some real sense a terraqueous globe. Where snows melt there must be water; and the origin of the Rhone from a great glacier is scarcely more evident to our senses than the dissolution of the Martian ice-caps into pools and streams.'

### PLATE XXI.

Chart of Mars. 'Memoirs of the British Astronomical Association,' Vol. XI., Part III., Plate VI.

Closely linked with the question of the existence of water on the planet, and indeed a fundamental point in the settlement of it, is the further question of whether there is any aqueous vapour in the Martian atmosphere. The evidence is somewhat conflicting. It is quite apparent that in the atmosphere of Mars there is nothing like the volume of water vapour which is present in that of the earth, for if there were, his features would be much more frequently obscured by cloud than is found to be the case. Still there are many observations on record which seem quite unaccountable unless the occasional presence of clouds is allowed. Thus on May 21, 1903, Mr. Denning records that the Syrtis Major (see Chart, Plate XXI.) being then very dark and sharply outlined, a very bright region crossed its southern extremity. By May 23, the Syrtis Major, 'usually the most conspicuous object in Mars, had become extremely feeble, as if covered with highly reflective vapours.' On May 24, Mr. Phillips observed the region of Zephyria and Aeolis to be also whitened, while the Syrtis Major was very faint; and on the 25th, Mr. Denning observed the striking whiteness of the same region observed by Mr. Phillips the day before. Illusion, so often invoked to explain away inconvenient observations, seems here impossible, in view of the prominence of the markings obscured, and the experience of the observers; and the evidence seems strongly in favour of real obscuration by cloud. It might have been expected that the evidence of the spectroscope would in such a case be decisive, but Campbell's negative conclusion is balanced by the affirmative result reached by Huggins and Vogel. It is safe to say, however, that whatever be the constitution of the Martian atmosphere, it is considerably less dense than our own air mantle.

During the last few years the public mind has been unusually exercised over Mars, largely by reason of a misapprehension of the terms employed in the discussion about his physical features. The talk of 'canals' has suggested human, or at all events intelligent, agency, and the expectation arose that it might not be quite impossible to establish communication between our world and its nearest neighbour on the further side. The idea is, of course, only an old one furbished up again, for early in last century it was suggested that a huge triangle or ellipse should be erected on the Siberian steppes to show the Lunarians or the Martians that we were intelligent creatures who knew geometry. In these circumstances curiosity was whetted by the announcement, first made in 1890, and since frequently repeated, of the appearance of bright projections on the terminator of Mars. These were construed, by people with vivid imaginations, as signals from the Martians to us; while a popular novelist suggested a more sinister interpretation, and harrowed our feelings with weird descriptions of the invasion of our world by Martian beings of uncouth appearance and superhuman intelligence, who were shot to our globe by an immense gun whose flashes occasioned the bright projections seen. The projections were, however, prosaically referred by Campbell to snow-covered mountains, while Lowell believed that one very large one observed at Flagstaff in May, 1903, was due to sunlight striking on a great cloud, not of water-vapour, but of dust.

As a matter of fact, Mars is somewhat disappointing to those who approach the study of his surface with the hope of finding traces of anything which might favour the idea of human habitation. He presents an apparently enticing general resemblance to the earth, with his polar caps and his bright and dark markings; and his curious network of canals may suggest intelligent agency. But the resemblances are not nearly so striking when examined in detail. The polar caps are the only features that seem to hold their own beside their terrestrial analogues, and even their resemblance is not unquestioned; the dark areas, so long thought to be seas, are now proved to be certainly not seas, whatever else they may be; and the canal system presents nothing but the name of similarity to anything that we know upon earth. It is quite probable that were Mars to come as near to us as our own moon, the fancied resemblances would disappear almost entirely, and we should find that the red planet is only another instance of the infinite variety which seems to prevail among celestial bodies. That being so, it need scarcely be remarked that any talk about Martian inhabitants is, to say the least of it, premature. There may be such creatures, and they may be anything you like to imagine. There is no restraint upon the fancy, for no one knows anything about them, and no one is in the least likely to know anything.

The moons of Mars are among the most curious finds of modern astronomy. When the ingenious Dr. Jonathan Swift, in editing the travels of Mr. Lemuel Gulliver, of Wapping, wrote that the astronomers of Laputa had discovered 'two lesser stars, or satellites, which revolve about Mars,' the suggestion was, no doubt, put in merely because some detail of their skill had to be given, and as well one unlikely thing as another. Probably no one would have been more surprised than the Dean of St. Patrick's, had he lived long enough, or cared sixpence about the matter, to hear that his bow drawn at a venture had hit the mark, and that Professor Asaph Hall had detected two satellites of Mars. The discovery was one of the first-fruits of the 26-inch Washington refractor, and was made in 1877, the year from which the new interest in Mars may be said to date. The two moons have been called Deimos and Phobos, or Fear and Panic, and are, in all probability, among the very tiniest bodies of our system, as their diameter can scarcely be greater than ten miles. Deimos revolves in an orbit which takes him thirty hours eighteen minutes to complete, at a distance of 14,600 miles from the centre of Mars. Phobos is much nearer the planet, his distance from its centre being 5,800, while from its surface he is distant only 3,700 miles. In consequence of this nearness, he can never be seen by an observer on Mars from any latitude higher than 69°, the bulge of the globe permanently shutting him out from view. His period of revolution is only seven hours thirty-nine minutes, so that to the Martian inhabitants, if there are any, the nearer of the planet's moons must appear to rise in the west and set in the east. By the combination of its own revolution and the opposite rotation of Mars it will take about eleven hours to cross the heavens; and during that period it will go through all its phases and half through a second display.

These little moons are certainly among the most curious and interesting bodies of the solar system; but, unfortunately, the sight of them is denied to most observers. That they were not seen by Sir William Herschel with his great 4-foot reflector probably only points to the superior defining power of the 26-inch Washington refractor as compared with Herschel's celebrated but cumbrous instrument. Still, they were missed by many telescopes quite competent to show them, and of as good defining quality as the Washington instrument—a fact which goes to add proof, if proof were needed, that the power which makes discoveries is the product of telescope × observer, and that of the two factors concerned the latter is the more important. It is said that the moons have been seen by Dr. Wentworth Erck with a 7⅓-inch refractor. The ordinary observer is not likely to catch even a glimpse of them with anything much smaller than a 12-inch instrument, and even then must use precautions to exclude the glare of the planet, and may count himself lucky if he succeed in the observation.

A word or two may be said as to what a beginner may expect to see with a small instrument. It has been stated that nothing under 6 inches can make much of Mars; but this is a somewhat exaggerated statement of the case. It is quite certain that the bulk of the more prominent markings can be seen with telescopes of much smaller aperture. Some detail has been seen with only 1¾-inch, while Grover has, with a 2-inch, executed drawings which show how much can be done with but little telescopic power. The fact is, that observers who are only in the habit of using large telescopes are apt to be unduly sceptical of the powers of small ones, which are often wonderfully efficient. The fine detail of the canal system is, of course, altogether beyond small instruments; and, generally speaking, it will take at least a 4-inch to show even the more strongly marked of these strange features. At the 1894 opposition, the writer, using a 3⅞-inch Dollond of good quality, was able to detect several of the more prominent canals, but only on occasions of the best definition. The accompanying rough sketch (Fig. 24) gives an idea of what may be expected to be seen, under favourable conditions, with an instrument of between 2 and 3 inches. It represents Mars as seen with a glass of 2⅝-inch aperture and fair quality. The main marking in the centre of the disc is that formerly known as the Kaiser or Hour-glass Sea. Its name in Schiaparelli's nomenclature, now universally used, is the Syrtis Major. The same marking will also be seen in Mr. Phillips's drawing of 1899, January 30, in which it is separated by a curious bright bridge from the Nilosyrtis to the North. The observer need scarcely expect to see much more than is depicted in Fig. 24, with an instrument of the class mentioned, but Plate XX. will give a very good idea of the appearance of the planet when viewed with a telescope of considerable power. The polar caps will be within reach, and sometimes present the effect of projecting above the general level of the planet's surface, owing, no doubt, to irradiation.

FIG. 24.

Mars, June 25, 1890, 10 hours 15 minutes; 2⅜-inch, power 120.

To the intending observer one important caution may be suggested. In observing and sketching the surface of Mars, do so *independently*. The chart which accompanies this chapter is given for the purpose of identifying markings which have been already seen, not for that of enabling the observer to see details which are beyond the power of his glass. No planet has been the cause of more illusion than Mars, and drawings of him are extant which resemble nothing so much as the photograph of an umbrella which has been turned inside out by a gust of wind. In such cases it may reasonably be concluded that there is something wrong, and that, unconsciously, 'the vision and the faculty divine' have been exercised at the expense of the more prosaic, but in this case more useful, quality of accuracy. By prolonged study of a modern chart of Mars, and a little gentle stretching of the imagination, the most unskilled observer with the smallest instrument will detect a multitude of canals upon the planet, to which there is but one objection, that they do not exist. There is enough genuine interest about Mars, even when viewed with a small glass, without the importation of anything spurious. In observation it will be noticed that as the rotation period of Mars nearly coincides with that of the earth, the change in the aspect presented from night to night will be comparatively small, the same object coming to the meridian thirty-seven minutes later each successive evening. Generally speaking, Mars is an easier object to define than either Venus or Jupiter, though perhaps scarcely bearing high powers so well as Saturn. There is no planet more certain to repay study and to maintain interest. He and Jupiter may be said to be at present the 'live' planets of the solar system in an astronomical sense.

---

\* The opposition of a planet occurs 'whenever the sun, the earth, and the planet, as represented in their projected orbits, are in a straight line, with the earth in the middle.'

† That point in the orbit of a planet or comet which is nearest to the sun.

# CHAPTER IX

## THE ASTEROIDS

In the year 1772 Bode of Berlin published the statement of a curiously symmetrical relation existing among the planets of our system. The gist of this relation, known as Bode's law, though it was really discovered by Titius of Wittenberg, may be summed up briefly thus: 'The interval between the orbits of any two planets is about twice as great as the inferior interval, and only half the superior one.' Thus the distance between the orbits of the earth and Venus should, according to Bode's law, be half of that between the earth and Mars, which again should be half of that which separates Mars from the planet next beyond him. Since the discovery of Neptune, this so-called law has broken down, for Neptune is very far within the distance which it requires; but at the time of its promulgation it represented with considerable accuracy the actual relative positions of the planets, with one exception. Between Mars and Jupiter there was a blank which should, according to the law, have been filled by a planet, but to all appearance was not. Noticing this blank in the sequence, Bode ventured to predict that a planet would be found to fill it; and his foresight was not long in being vindicated.

Several continental astronomers formed a kind of planet-hunting society to look out for the missing orb; but their operations were anticipated by the discovery on January 1, 1801, of a small planet which occupied a place closely approximating to that indicated for the missing body by Bode's law. The news of this discovery, made by Piazzi of Palermo in the course of observations for his well-known catalogue of stars, did not reach Bode till March 20, and 'the delay just afforded time for the publication, by a young philosopher of Jena named Hegel, of a "Dissertation" showing, by the clearest light of reason, that the number of the planets could not exceed seven, and exposing the folly of certain devotees of induction who sought a new celestial body merely to fill a gap in a numerical series.'

The remarkable agreement of prediction and discovery roused a considerable amount of interest, though the planet actually found, and named Ceres after the patron-goddess of Sicily, seemed disappointingly small. But before very long Olbers, one of the members of the original planet-hunting society, surprised the astronomical world by the discovery of a second planet which also fulfilled the condition of Bode's law; and by the end of March, 1807, two other planets equally obedient to the required numerical standard were found, the first by Harding, the second by Olbers. Thus a system of four small planets, Ceres, Pallas, Juno, and Vesta, was found to fill that gap in the series which had originally suggested the search. To account for their existence Olbers proposed the theory that they were the fragments of a large planet which had been blown to pieces either by the disruptive action of internal forces or by collision with a comet; and this theory remained in favour for a number of years, though accumulating evidence against it has forced its abandonment.

It was not till 1845 that there was any addition to the number of the asteroids, as they had come to be named. In that year, however, Hencke of Driessen in Prussia, discovered a fifth, which has been named Astræa, and in 1847 repeated his success by the discovery of a sixth, Hebe. Since that time there has been a steady flow of discoveries, until at the present time the number known to exist is close upon 700, of which 569 have received permanent numbers as undoubtedly distinct members of the solar system; and this total is being steadily added to year by year, the average annual number of discoveries for the years 1902 to 1905 inclusive, being fifty-two. For a time the search for minor planets was a most laborious business. The planet-hunter had to construct careful maps of all the stars visible in a certain small zone of the ecliptic, and to compare these methodically with the actual face of the sky in the same zone, as revealed by his telescope. Any star seen in the telescope, and not found to be marked upon the chart, became forthwith an object of grave suspicion, and was watched until its motion, or lack of motion, relatively to the other stars either proved or disproved its planetary nature. At present this lengthy and wearisome process has been entirely superseded by the photographic method, in which a minor planet is detected by the fact that, being in motion relatively to the fixed stars, its image will appear upon the plate in the shape of a short line or trail, the images of the fixed stars being round dots. Of course the trail may be due to a planet which has already been discovered; but should there be no known minor planet in the position occupied by the trail, then a new member has been added to the system. Minor-planet hunting has always been a highly specialized branch of astronomy, and a few observers, such as Peters, Watson, Charlois and Palisa, and at present Wolf, have accounted for the great majority of the discoveries.

It was, however, becoming more and more a matter of question what advantage was to be gained by the continuance of the hunt, when a fresh fillip was given to interest by the discovery in 1898 of the anomalous asteroid named Eros. Hitherto no minor planet had been known to have the greater portion of its orbit within that of Mars, though several do cross the red planet's borders; but the mean distance of Eros from the sun proves to be about 135,000,000, while that of Mars is 141,000,000 miles. In addition, the orbit of the new planet is such that at intervals of sixty-seven years it comes within 15,000,000 miles of the earth, or in other words nearer to us than any other celestial body except the moon or a chance comet. It may thus come to afford a means of revising estimates of celestial distances. Eros presents another peculiarity. It has been found by E. von Oppolzer to be variable in a period of two hours thirty-eight minutes; and the theory has been put forward that the planet is double, consisting of two bodies which revolve almost in contact and mutually eclipse one another—in short, that Eros as a planet presents the same phenomenon which we shall find as a characteristic of that type of variable stars known as the Algol type. An explanation, in some respects more simple and satisfactory, is that the variation in light is caused by the different reflective power of various parts of its surface; but the question is still open.

The best results for the sizes of the four asteroids first discovered are those of Barnard, from direct measurements with the Lick telescope in 1894. He found the diameter of Ceres to be 485 miles, that of Pallas 304, those of Vesta and Juno 243 and 118 miles respectively. There appears to be as great diversity in the reflective power of these original members of the group as in their diameters. Ceres is large and dull, and, in Miss Clerke's words, 'must be composed of rugged and sombre rock, unclothed probably by any vestige of air,' while Vesta has a surface which reflects light with four times the intensity of that of Ceres, and is, in fact, almost as brilliantly white as newly fallen snow.

In the place of Olbers' discredited hypothesis of an exploded planet, has now been set the theory first suggested by Kirkwood, that instead of having in the asteroids the remnants of a world which has become defunct, we have the materials of one which was never allowed to form, the overwhelming power of Jupiter's attraction having exerted a disruptive influence over them while their formation was still only beginning.

So far as I am aware, they share with Mars the distinction of being the only celestial bodies which have been made the subjects of a testamentary disposition. In the case of Mars, readers may remember that some years ago a French lady left a large sum of money to be given to the individual who should first succeed in establishing communication with the Planet of War; in that of the asteroids, the late Professor Watson, a mighty hunter of minor planets in his day, made provision for the supervision of the twenty-two planets captured by him, lest any of them should get lost, stolen, or strayed.

Small telescopes are, of course, quite impotent to deal with such diminutive bodies as the asteroids; nor, perhaps, is it desirable that the ranks of the minor-planet hunters should be reinforced to any extent.

# CHAPTER X

## JUPITER

Passing outwards from the zone of the minor planets, we come to the greatest and most magnificent member of the solar system, the giant planet Jupiter. To most observers, Jupiter will probably appear not only the largest, but also the most interesting telescopic object which our system affords. Some, no doubt, will put in a claim for Mars, and some will share Sir Robert Ball's predilection for Saturn; but the interest attaching to Mars is of quite a different character from that which belongs to Jupiter, and while Saturn affords a picture of unsurpassed beauty, there is not that interest of variety and change in his exquisite system which is to be found in that of his neighbour planet. Jupiter is constantly attractive by reason of the hope, or rather the certainty, that he will always provide something fresh to observe; and the perpetual state of flux in which the details of his surface present themselves to the student offers to us the only instance which can be conveniently inspected of the process of world-formation. Jupiter is at the very opposite end of the scale from such a body, for example, as our own moon. On the latter it would appear as though all things were approaching the fixity of death; such changes as are suspected are scarcely more than suspected, and, even if established, are comparatively so small as to tax the utmost resources of observation. On the former, such a thing as fixity or stability appears to be unknown, and changes are constantly occurring on a scale so gigantic as not to be beyond the reach of small instruments, at least in their broader outlines.

The main facts relating to the planet may be briefly given before we go on to consider the physical features revealed to us by the telescope. Jupiter then travels round the sun in a period of 11 years, 314·9 days, at an average distance of almost 483,000,000 miles. According to Barnard's measures, his polar diameter is 84,570, and his equatorial diameter 90,190 miles. He is thus compressed at the poles to the extent of $^1/_{16}$, and there is no planet which so conspicuously exhibits to the eye the actual effect of this polar flattening, though the compression of Saturn is really greater still. In volume he is equal to more than 1,300 earths, but his density is so small that only 316 of our worlds would be needed to balance him. This low density, not much greater than that of water, is quite in accordance with all the other features which are revealed by observation, and appears to be common to all the members of that group of large exterior planets of which Jupiter is at once the first and the chief.

The brilliancy of the great planet is exceedingly remarkable, far exceeding that of Mars or Saturn, and only yielding to that of Venus. In 1892 his lustre was double that of Sirius, which is by far the brightest of all the fixed stars; and he has been repeatedly seen by the unaided eye even when the sun was above the horizon. According to one determination he reflects practically the same amount of light as newly fallen snow; and even if this be rejected as impossibly high, Zöllner's more moderate estimate, which puts his reflective power at 62 per cent. of the light received, makes him almost as bright as white paper. Yet to the eye it is very evident that his light has a distinct golden tinge, and in the telescopic view this remains conspicuous, and is further emphasized by the presence on his disc of a considerable variety of colouring.

Under favourable circumstances Jupiter presents to us a disc which measures as much as 50″ in diameter. The very low magnifying power of 50 will therefore present him to the eye with a diameter of 2,500″, which is somewhat greater than the apparent diameter of the moon. In practice it is somewhat difficult to realize that this is the case, probably owing to the want of any other object in the telescopic field with which to compare the planet. But while there may be a little disappointment at the seeming smallness of the disc even with a power double that suggested, this will quickly be superseded by a growing interest in the remarkable picture which is revealed to view.

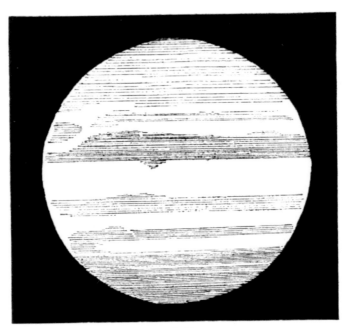

FIG. 25.

JUPITER, October 9, 1891, 9.30 p.m.; 3⅞-inch, power 120.

Some idea of the ordinary appearance of the planet may be gained from Fig. 25, which reproduces a sketch made with a small telescope on October 9, 1891. The first feature that strikes the eye on even the most casual glance is the polar compression. The outline of the disc is manifestly not circular but elliptical, and this is emphasized by the fact that nearly all the markings which are visible run parallel to one another in the direction of the longest diameter of the oval. A little attention will reveal these markings as a series of dark shadowy bands, of various breadths and various tones, which stretch from side to side of the disc, fading a little in intensity as they approach its margin, and giving the whole planet the appearance of being girdled by a number of cloudy belts. The belts may be seen with very low powers indeed, the presence of the more conspicuous ones having repeatedly been evident to the writer with the rudimentary telescope mentioned in Chapter II., consisting of a non-achromatic double convex lens of 1½-inch aperture, and a single lens eye-piece giving a power of 36. Anything larger and more perfect than this will bring them out with clearness, and an achromatic of from 2 to 3 inches aperture will give views of the highest beauty and interest, and will even enable its possessor to detect some of the more prominent evidences of the changes which are constantly taking place.

The number of belts visible varies very considerably. As many as thirty have sometimes been counted; but normally the number is much smaller than this. Speaking generally, two belts, one on either side of a bright equatorial zone, will be found to be conspicuous, while fainter rulings may be traced further north and south, and the dusky hoods which cover the poles will be almost as easily seen as the two main belts. It will further become apparent that this system of markings is characterized by great variety of colouring. In this respect no planet approaches Jupiter, and when seen under favourable circumstances and with a good instrument, preferably a reflector, some of the colour effects are most exquisite. Webb remarks: 'There is often "something rich and strange" in the colouring of the disc. Lord Rosse describes yellow, brick-red, bluish, and even full-blue markings; Hirst, a belt edged with crimson lake; Miss Hirst, a small sea-green patch near one of the poles.' The following notes of colour were made on December 26, 1905: The south equatorial belt distinct reddish-brown; the equatorial zone very pale yellow, almost white, with faint slaty-blue shades in the northern portion; the north polar regions a decided reddish-orange; while the south polar hood was of a much colder greyish tone. But the colours are subject to considerable change, and the variations of the two great equatorial belts appear, according to Stanley Williams, to be periodic, maxima and minima of redness being separated by a period of about twelve years, and the maximum of the one belt coinciding with the minimum of the other.

**PLATE XXII.**

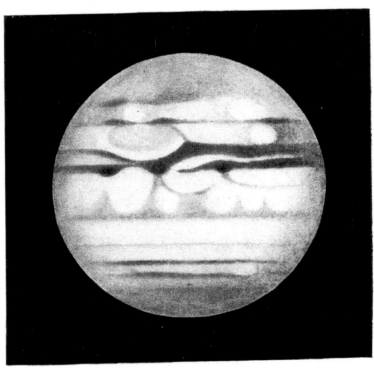

Jupiter, January 6, 1906—8 hours 20 minutes. Instrument, 9¼-inch Reflector.
λ = 238° (System 1); λ = 55° (System 2).

Rev. T. E. R. Phillips.

These changes in colouring bring us to the fact that the whole system of the Jovian markings is liable to constant and often very rapid change. Anyone who compares drawings made a few years ago with those made at the present time, such as Plates XXII. and XXIII., cannot fail to notice that while there is a general similarity, the details have changed so much that there is scarcely one individual feature which has not undergone some modification. Indeed, this process of change is sometimes so rapid that it can be actually watched in its occurrence. Thus Mr. Denning remarks that 'on October 17, 1880, two dark spots, separated by 20° of longitude, broke out on a belt some 25° north of the equator. Other spots quickly formed on each side of the pair alluded to, and distributed themselves along the belt, so that by December 30 they covered three-fourths of its entire circumference.' The dark belts, according to his observations, 'appear to be sustained in certain cases by eruptions of dark matter, which gradually spread out into streams.'

Even the great equatorial belts are not exempt from the continual flux which affects all the markings of the great planet, and the details of their structure will be found to vary to a considerable extent at different periods. At present the southern belt is by far the most conspicuous feature of the surface, overpowering all other details by its prominence, while its northern rival has shrunk in visibility to a mere shadow of what it appears in drawings made in the seventies. Through all the changes of the last thirty years, however, one very remarkable feature of the planet has remained permanent at least in form, though varying much in visibility. With the exception of the canals of Mars, no feature of any of the planets has excited so much interest as the great red spot on Jupiter. The history of this extraordinary phenomenon as a subject of general study begins in 1878, though records exist as far back as 1869 of a feature which almost certainly was the same, and it has been suggested that it was observed by Cassini two centuries ago. In 1878 it began to attract general attention, which it well deserved. In appearance it was an enormous ellipse of a full brick-red colour, measuring some 30,000 miles in length by 7,000 in breadth, and lying immediately south of the south equatorial belt. With this belt it appears to have some mysterious connection. It is not actually joined to it, but seems, as Miss Clerke observes, to be 'jammed down upon it'; at least, in the south equatorial belt, just below where the spot lies, there has been formed an enormous bay, bounded on the following side (*i.e.*, the right hand as the planet moves through the field), by a sharply upstanding shoulder or cape. The whole appearance of this bay irresistibly suggests to the observer that it has somehow or other been hollowed out to make room for the spot, which floats, as it were, within it, surrounded generally by a margin of bright material, which divides it from the brown matter of the belt. The red spot, with its accompanying bay and cape, is shown in Fig. 25 and in Plate XXII., which represents the planet as seen by the Rev. T. E. R. Phillips on January 6, 1906. The spot has varied very much in colour and in visibility, but on the whole its story has been one of gradual decline; its tint has paled, and its outline has become less distinct, as though it were being obscured by an outflow of lighter-coloured matter, though there have been occasional recoveries both of colour and distinctness. In 1891 it was a perfectly easy object with 3⅞ inches; at the present time the writer has never found it anything but difficult with an 18-inch aperture, though some observers have been able to see it steadily in 1905 and 1906 with much smaller telescopes. The continued existence of the bay already referred to seems to indicate that it is only the colour of the spot that has temporarily paled, and that observers may in course of time witness a fresh development of this most interesting Jovian feature.

The nature of the red spot remains an enigma. It may possibly represent an opening in the upper strata of Jupiter's dense cloud-envelope, through which lower strata, or even the real body of the planet, may be seen. The suggestion has also been made that it is the glow of some volcanic fire on the body of the planet, seen through the cloud-screen as the light of a lamp is seen through ground-glass. But, after all, such ideas are only conjectures, and it is impossible to say as yet even whether the spot is higher or lower than the average level of the surface round it. A curious phenomenon which was witnessed in 1891 suggested at first a hope that this question of relative height would at least be determined. This phenomenon was the overtaking of the red spot by a dark spot which had been travelling after it on the same parallel, but with greater speed, for some months. It appeared to be quite certain that the dark spot must either transit the face of the red spot or else pass behind it; and in either case interesting information as to the relative elevations of the two features in question would have been obtained. The dark spot, however, disappointed expectation by drifting round the south margin of the red one, much as the current of a river is turned aside by the buttress of a bridge. In fact, it would almost appear as though the red spot had the power of resisting any pressure from other parts of the planet's surface; yet in itself it has no fixity, for its period of rotation steadily lengthened for several years until 1899, since when it has begun to shorten again, so that it would appear to float upon the surface of currents of variable speed rather than to be an established landmark of the globe itself. The rotation period derived from it was, in 1902, 9 hours 55 minutes 39·3 seconds.

The mention of the changing period of rotation of the red spot lends emphasis to the fact that no single period of rotation can be assigned to Jupiter as a whole. It is impossible to say of the great planet that he rotates in such and such a period: the utmost that can be said is that certain spots upon his surface have certain rotation periods; but these periods are almost all different from one another, and even the period of an individual marking is subject, as already seen, to variation. In fact, as Mr. Stanley Williams has shown, no fewer than nine different periods of rotation are found to coexist upon the surface; and though the differences in the periods seem small when expressed in time, amounting in the extreme cases only to eight and half minutes, yet their significance is very great indeed. In the case of Mr. Williams's Zones II. and III., the difference in speed of these two surface currents amounts to 400 miles per hour. Certain bright spots near the equator have been found to move so much more rapidly than the great red spot as to pass it at a speed of 260 miles an hour, and to 'lap' it in forty-four and a half days, completing in that time one whole rotation more than their more imposing neighbour. It cannot, therefore, be said that Jupiter's rotation period is known; but the average period of his surface markings is somewhere about nine hours fifty-two minutes.

Thus the rotation period adds its evidence to that already afforded by the variations in colour and in form of the planet's markings that here we are dealing with a body in a very different condition from that of any of the other members of our system hitherto met with. We have here no globe whose actual surface we can scrutinize, as we can in the case of Mars and the moon, but one whose solid nucleus, if it has such a thing, is perpetually veiled from us by a mantle which seems more akin to the photosphere of the sun than to anything else that we are acquainted with. The obvious resemblances may, and very probably do, mask quite as important differences. The mere difference in scale between the two bodies concerned must be a very important factor, to say nothing of other causes which may be operative in producing unlikeness. Still, there is a considerable and suggestive general resemblance.

In the sun and in Jupiter alike we have a view, not of the true surface, but of an envelope which seems to represent the point of condensation of currents of matter thrown up from depths below—an envelope agitated in both cases, though more slowly in that of Jupiter, by disturbances which bear witness to the operation of stupendous forces beneath its veil. In both bodies there is a similar small density: neither the sun nor Jupiter is much denser than water; in both the determination of the rotation period is complicated by the fact that the markings of the bright envelope by which the determinations must be made move with entirely different speeds in different latitudes. Here, however, there is a divergence, for while in the case of the sun the period increases uniformly from the equator to the poles, there is no such uniformity in the case of Jupiter. Thus certain dark spots in 25° north latitude were found in 1880 to have a shorter period than even the swift equatorial white markings.

One further circumstance remains to be noted in pursuance of these resemblances. Not only does the disc of Jupiter shade away at its edges in a manner somewhat similar to that of the sun, being much more brilliant in the centre than at the limb, but his remarkable brilliancy, already noticed, has given rise to the suggestion that to some small extent he may shine by his own inherent light. There are certain difficulties, however, in the way of such a suggestion. The satellites, for example, disappear absolutely when they enter the shadow of their great primary—a fact which is conclusive against the latter being self-luminous to anything more than a very small extent, as even a small emission of native light from Jupiter would suffice to render them visible. But even supposing that the idea of self-luminosity has to be abandoned, everything points to the fact that in Jupiter we have a body which presents much stronger analogies to the sun than to those planets of the solar system which we have so far considered. The late Mr. R. A. Proctor's conclusion probably represents the true state of the case with regard to the giant planet: 'It may be regarded as practically proved that Jupiter's condition rather resembles that of a small sun which has nearly reached the dark stage than that of a world which is within a measurable time-interval from the stage of orb-life through which our own Earth is passing.'

Leaving the planet itself, we turn to the beautiful system of satellites of which it is the centre. The four moons which, till 1892, were thought to compose the complete retinue of Jupiter, were among the first-fruits of Galileo's newly-invented telescope, and were discovered in January, 1610. The names attached to them—Io, Europa, Ganymede, and Callisto—have now been almost discarded in favour of the more prosaic but more convenient numbers I., II., III., IV. The question of their visibility to the unaided eye has been frequently discussed, but with little result; nor is it a matter of much importance whether or not some person exceptionally gifted with keenness of sight may succeed in catching a momentary glimpse of one which happens to be favourably placed. The smallest telescope or a field-glass will show them quite clearly. They are, in fact, bodies of considerable size, III., which is the largest, being 3,558 miles in diameter, while IV. is only about 200 miles less; and a moderate magnifying power will bring out their discs.

**PLATE XXIII.**

Jupiter, February 17, 1906. J. Baikie, 18-inch Reflector.

The beautiful symmetry of this miniature system was broken in 1892 by Barnard's discovery of a fifth satellite—so small and so close to the great planet that very few telescopes are of power sufficient to show it. This was followed in 1904 by Perrine's discovery, from photographs taken at the Lick Observatory with the Crossley reflector, of two more members of the system, so that the train of Jupiter as at present known numbers seven. The fifth, sixth, and seventh satellites are, of course, far beyond the powers of any but the very finest instruments, their diameters being estimated at 120, 100, and 30 miles respectively. It will be a matter of interest, however, for the observer to follow the four larger satellites, and to watch their rapid relative changes of position; their occultations, when they pass behind the globe of Jupiter; their eclipses, when they enter the great cone of shadow which the giant planet casts behind him into space; and, most beautiful of all, their transits. In occultations the curious phenomenon is sometimes witnessed of an apparent flattening of the planet's margin as the satellite approaches it at ingress or draws away from it at egress. This strange optical illusion, which also occurs occasionally in the case of transits, was witnessed by several observers on various dates during the winter of 1905-1906. It is, of course, merely an illusion, but it is curious why it should happen on some occasions and not on others, when to all appearance the seeing is of very much the same quality. The gradual fading away of the light of the satellites as they enter into eclipse is also a very interesting feature, but the transits are certainly the most beautiful objects of all for a small instrument. The times of all these events are given in such publications as the 'Nautical Almanac' or the 'Companion to the Observatory'; but should the student not be possessed of either of these most useful publications, he may notice that when a satellite is seen steadily approaching Jupiter on the following side, a transit is impending. The satellite will come up to the margin of the planet, looking like a brilliant little bead of light as it joins itself to it (a particularly exquisite sight), will glide across the margin, and after a longer or shorter period will become invisible, being merged in the greater brightness of the central portions of Jupiter's disc, unless it should happen to traverse one of the dark belts, in which case it may be visible throughout its entire journey. It will be followed or preceded, according to the season, by its shadow, which will generally appear as a dark circular dot. In transits which occur before opposition the shadows precede the satellites; after opposition they travel behind them. The transit of the satellite itself will in most cases be a pretty sharp test of the performance of a 3-inch telescope, or anything below that aperture; but the transit of the shadow may be readily seen with a 2½-inch, probably even with a 2-inch. There are certain anomalies in the behaviour of the shadows which have never been satisfactorily explained. They have not always been seen of a truly circular form, nor always of the same degree of darkness, that of the second satellite being notably lighter in most instances than those of the others. There are few more beautiful celestial pictures than that presented by Jupiter with a satellite and its shadow in transit. The swift rotation of the great planet and the rapid motion of the shadow can be very readily observed, and the whole affords a most picturesque illustration of celestial mechanics.

A few notes may be added with regard to observation. In drawing the planet regard must first of all be paid to the fact that Jupiter's disc is not circular, and should never be so represented. It is easy for the student to prepare for himself a disc of convenient size, say about 2½ inches in diameter on the major axis, and compressed to the proper extent ($\frac{1}{16}$), which may be used in outlining all subsequent drawings. Within the outline thus sketched the details must be drawn with as great rapidity as is consistent with accuracy. The reason for rapidity will soon become obvious. Jupiter's period of rotation is so short that the aspect of his disc will be found to change materially even in half an hour. Indeed, twenty minutes is perhaps as long as the observer should allow himself for any individual drawing, and a little practice will convince him that it is quite possible to represent a good deal of detail in that time, and that, even with rapid work, the placing of the various markings may be made pretty accurate. The darker and more conspicuous features should be laid down first of all, and the more delicate details thereafter filled in, care being taken to secure first those near the preceding margin of the planet before they are carried out of view by rotation. The colours of the various features should be carefully noted at the sides of the original drawings, and for this work twilight observations are to be preferred.

Different observers vary to some extent, as might be expected, in their estimates of the planet's colouring, but on the whole there is a broad general agreement. No planet presents such a fine opportunity for colour-study as Jupiter, and on occasions of good seeing the richness of the tones is perfectly astonishing. In showing the natural colours of the planet the reflector has a great advantage over the refractor, and observers using the reflecting type of instrument should devote particular attention to this branch of the subject, as there is no doubt that the colour of the various features is liable to considerable, perhaps seasonal, variation, and systematic observation of its changes may prove helpful in solving the mystery of Jupiter's condition. The times of beginning and ending observation should be carefully noted, and also the magnifying powers employed. These should not be too high. Jupiter does not need, and will not stand, so much enlargement as either Mars or Saturn. It is quite easy to secure a very large disc, but over-magnifying is a great deal worse than useless: it is a fertile source of mistakes and illusions. If the student be content to make reasonable use of his means, and not to overpress either his instrument or his imagination, he will find upon Jupiter work full of absorbing interest, and may be able to make his own contribution to the serious study of the great planet.

# CHAPTER XI

## SATURN

At nearly double the distance of Jupiter from the sun circles the second largest planet of our system, unique, so far as human knowledge goes, in the character of its appendages. The orbit of Saturn has a mean radius of 886,000,000 miles, but owing to its eccentricity, his distance may be diminished to 841,000,000 or increased to 931,000,000. This large variation may not play so important a part in his economy as might have been supposed, owing to the fact that the sun heat received by him is not much more than $\frac{1}{100}$th of that received by the earth. The planet occupies twenty-nine and a half years in travelling round its immense orbit. Barnard's measures with the Lick telescope give for the polar diameter 69,770, and for the equatorial 76,470 miles. Saturn's polar compression is accordingly very great, amounting to about $\frac{1}{12}$th. Generally speaking, however, it is not so obvious in the telescopic view as the smaller compression of Jupiter, being masked by the proximity of the rings.

### PLATE XXIV.

Saturn, July 2, 1894. E. E. Barnard, 36-inch Equatorial.

Saturn is the least dense of all the planets; in fact, this enormous globe, nine times the diameter of the earth, would float in water. This fact of extremely low density at once suggests a state of matters similar to that already seen to exist, in all likelihood, in the case of Jupiter; and all the evidence goes to support the view that Saturn, along with the other three large exterior planets, is in the condition of a semi-sun.

The globe presents, on the whole, similar characteristics to those already noticed as prevailing on Jupiter, but, as was to be expected, in a condition enfeebled by the much greater distance across which they are viewed and the smaller scale on which they are exhibited. It is generally girdled by one or two tropical belts of a grey-green tone; the equatorial region is yellow, and sometimes, like the corresponding region of Jupiter, bears light spots upon it and a narrow equatorial band of a dusky tone; the polar regions are of a cold ashy or leaden colour. Professor Barnard's fine drawing (Plate XXIV.) gives an admirable representation of these features as seen with the 36-inch Lick telescope. Altogether, whether from greater distance or from intrinsic deficiency, the colouring of Saturn is by no means so vivid or so interesting as that of his larger neighbour.

The period of rotation was, till within the last few years, thought to be definitely and satisfactorily ascertained. Sir William Herschel fixed it, from his observations, at ten hours sixteen minutes. Professor Asaph Hall, from observations of a white spot near the equator, reduced this period to ten hours fourteen minutes twenty-four seconds. Stanley Williams and Denning, in 1891, reached results differing only by about two seconds from that of Hall; but the former, discussing observations of 1893, arrived at the conclusion that there were variations of rotation presented in different latitudes and longitudes of the planet's surface, the longest period being ten hours fifteen minutes, and the shortest ten hours twelve minutes forty-five seconds. Subsequently Keeler obtained, by spectroscopic methods, a result exactly agreeing with that of Hall. It appeared, therefore, that fairly satisfactory agreement had been reached on a mean period of ten hours fourteen minutes twenty-four seconds.

In 1903, however, a number of bright spots appeared in a middle north latitude which, when observed by Barnard, Comas Solà, Denning, and other observers, gave a period remarkably longer than that deduced from spots in lower latitudes—namely, about ten hours thirty-eight minutes. Accordingly, it follows that the surface of Saturn's equatorial regions rotates much more rapidly than that of the regions further north—a state of affairs which presents an obvious likeness to that prevailing on Jupiter. But in the case of Saturn the equatorial current must move relatively to the rest of the surface at the enormous rate of from 800 to 900 miles an hour, a speed between three and four times greater than that of the corresponding current on Jupiter!

The resemblance between the two great planets is thus very marked indeed. Great size, coupled with small density; very rapid rotation, with its accompaniment of large polar compression; and, even more markedly in the case of the more distant planet than in that of Jupiter, a variety of rotation periods for different markings, which indicates that these features have been thrown up from different strata of the planet's substance—such points of likeness are too significant to be ignored. It is not at all likely that Saturn has any solidity to speak of, any more than Jupiter; the probabilities all point in the direction of a comparatively small nucleus of somewhat greater solidity than the rest, surrounded by an immense condensation shell, where the products of various eruptions are represented.

Were this all that can be said about Saturn, the planet would scarcely be more than a reduced and somewhat less interesting edition of Jupiter. As it is, he possesses characteristics which make him Jupiter's rival in point of interest, and, as a mere telescopic picture, perhaps even his superior. When Galileo turned his telescope upon Saturn, he was presented with what seemed an insoluble enigma. It appeared to him that, instead of being a single globe, the planet consisted of three globes in contact with one another; and this supposed fact he intimated to Kepler in an anagram, which, when rearranged, read: 'Altissimum planetam tergeminum observavi'—'I have observed the most distant planet to be threefold.' Under better conditions of observation, he remarked subsequently, the planet appeared like an olive, as it still does with low powers. This was sufficiently puzzling, but worse was to follow. After an interval, on observing Saturn again, he found that the appearances which had so perplexed him had altogether disappeared; the globe was single, like those of the other planets. In his letter to Welser, dated December 4, 1612, the great astronomer describes his bewilderment, and his fear lest, after all, it should turn out that his adversaries had been right, and that his discoveries had been mere illusions.

Then followed a period when observers could only command optical power sufficient to show the puzzling nature of the planet's appendages, without revealing their true form. It appeared that Saturn had 'ansæ,' or handles, on either side of him, between which and his body the sky could be seen; and many uncouth figures are still preserved which eloquently testify to the bewilderment of those who drew them, though some of them are wonderfully accurate representations of the planet's appearance when seen with insufficient means. The bewilderment was sometimes veiled, in amusing cuttle-fish fashion, under an inky cloud of sesquipedalian words. Thus Hevelius describes the aspects of Saturn in the following blasting flight of projectiles: 'The mono-spherical, the tri-spherical, the spherico-ansated, the elliptico-ansated, and the spherico-cuspidated,' which is very beautiful no doubt, but scarcely so simple as one could wish a popular explanation to be.

In the year 1659, however, Huygens, who had been observing Saturn with a telescope of 2⅓ inches aperture and 23 feet focal length, bearing a magnifying power of 100, arrived at the correct solution of the mystery, which he announced to, or rather concealed from, the world in a barbarous jumble of letters, which, when properly arranged, read 'annulo cingitur, tenui, plano, nusquam cohaerente, ad eclipticam inclinato'—'he (Saturn) is surrounded by a thin flat ring, nowhere touching (him, and) inclined to the ecliptic.' Huygens also discovered the first and largest of Saturn's satellites, Titan. His discoveries were followed by those of Cassini, who in 1676 announced his observation of that division in the ring which now goes by his name. From Cassini's time onwards to the middle of the nineteenth century, nothing was observed to alter to any great extent the conception of the Saturnian system which had been reached; though certain observations were made, which, though viewed with some suspicion, seemed to indicate that there were more divisions in the ring than that which Cassini had discovered, and that the system was thus a multiple one. In particular a marking on the outer ring was detected by Encke, and named after him, though generally seen, if seen at all, rather as a faint shading than as a definite division. (It is not shown in Barnard's drawing, Plate XXIV.). But in 1850 came the last great addition to our knowledge of the ring system, W. C. Bond in America, and Dawes in England making independently the discovery of the faint third ring, known as the Crape Ring, which lies between the inner bright ring and the globe.

The extraordinary appendages thus gradually revealed present a constantly varying aspect according to the seasons of the long Saturnian year. At Saturn's equinoxes they disappear, being turned edgewise; then, reappearing, they gradually broaden until at the solstice, 7⅓ years later, they are seen at their widest expansion; while from this point they narrow again to the following equinox, and repeat the same process with the opposite side of the ring illuminated, the whole set of changes being gone through in 29 years 167·2 days. Barnard's measures give for the outer diameter of the outer ring 172,310 miles; while the clear interval between the inner margin of the Crape Ring and the ball is about 5,800 miles, and the width of the great division in the ring-system (Cassini's) 2,270 miles. In sharp contrast to these enormous figures is the fact that the rings have no measurable thickness at all, and can only be estimated at not more than 50 miles. They disappear absolutely when seen edgewise; even the great Lick telescope lost them altogether for three days in October, 1891.*

The answer to the question of what may be the constitution of these remarkable features may now be given with a moderate approach to certainty. It has been shown successively that the rings could not be solid, or liquid, and in 1857 Clerk-Maxwell demonstrated that the only possible constitution for such a body is that of an infinite number of small satellites. The rings of Saturn thus presumably consist of myriads of tiny moonlets, each pursuing its own individual orbit in its individual period, and all drawn to their present form of aggregation by the attraction of Saturn's bulging equator. The appearances presented by the rings are explicable on this theory, and on no other. Thus the brightness of the two rings A and B would arise from the closer grouping of the satellites within these zones; while the semi-darkness of the Crape Ring arises from the sparser sprinkling of the moonlets, which allows the dark sky to be seen between them. Cassini's division corresponds to a zone which has been deprived of satellites; and as it has been shown that this vacant zone occupies a position where a revolving body would be subject to disturbance from four of Saturn's satellites, the force which cleared this gap in the ring is obvious. It has been urged as an objection to the satellite theory that while the thin spreading of the moonlets would account for the comparative darkness of the Crape Ring when seen against the sky, it by no means accounts for the fact that this ring is seen as a dark stripe upon the body of the planet. Seeliger's explanation of this is both satisfactory and obvious, when once suggested—namely, that the darkness of the Crape Ring against the planet is due to the fact that what we see is not the actual transits of the satellites themselves, but the perpetual flitting of their shadows across the ball. The final and conclusive argument in favour of this theory of the constitution of the rings was supplied by the late Professor Keeler by means of the spectroscope. It is evident that if the rings were solid, the speed of rotation should increase from their inner to their outer margin—*i.e.*, the outer margin must move faster, in miles per second, than the inner does. If, on the contrary, the rings are composed of a great number of satellites, the relation will be exactly reversed, and, owing to the superior attractive force exercised upon them by the planet through their greater nearness to him, the inner satellites will revolve faster than the outer ones. Now, this point is capable of settlement by spectroscopic methods involving the application of the well-known Doppler's principle, that the speed of a body's motion produces definite and regular effects upon the pitch of the light emitted or reflected by it. The measurements were of extreme delicacy, but the result was to give a rate of motion of 12½ miles per second for the inner edge of ring B, and of 10 miles for the outer edge of A, thus affording unmistakable confirmation of the satellite theory of the rings. Keeler's results have since been confirmed by

119

Campbell and others; and it may be regarded as a demonstrated fact that the rings, as already stated, consist of a vast number of small satellites.

It has been maintained that the ball of Saturn is eccentrically placed within the ring, and further, that this eccentricity is essential to the stability of the system; while the suggestion has also been made that the ring-system is undergoing progressive change, and that the interval between it and the ball is lessening. It has to be noticed, however, that the best measures, those of Barnard, indicate that the ball is symmetrically placed within the rings; and the suggestion of a diminishing interval between the ring-system and the ball receives no countenance from comparison of the measures which have been made at different times.

There can be no question that of all objects presented to observation in the solar system, there is not one, which, for mere beauty and symmetry can be for a moment compared with Saturn, even though, as already indicated, Mars and Jupiter present features of more lasting interest. To quote Proctor's words: 'The golden disc, faintly striped with silver-tinted belts; the circling rings, with their various shades of brilliancy and colour; and the perfect symmetry of the system as it sweeps across the dark background of the field of view, combine to form a picture as charming as it is sublime and impressive.' Fortunately the main features of this beautiful picture are within the reach of very humble instruments. Webb states that when the ring system was at its greatest breadth he has seen it with a power of about twenty on only 1⅓-inch aperture. A beginner cannot expect to do so much with such small means; but at all events a 2-inch telescope with powers of from 50 to 100 will reveal the main outlines of the ring very well indeed, and, with careful attention will show the shadow of the ring upon the ball, and that of the ball upon the ring. When we come to the question of the division in the ring, we are on somewhat more doubtful ground. Proctor affirms that 'the division in the ring (Cassini's) can be seen in a good 2-inch aperture in favourable weather.' One would have felt inclined to say that the weather would require to be very favourable indeed, were it not that Proctor's statement is corroborated by Denning, who remarks that 'With a 2-inch refractor, power about ninety, not only are the rings splendidly visible, but Cassini's division is readily glimpsed, as well as the narrow dark belt on the body of the planet.' The student may, however, be warned against expecting that such statements will apply to his own individual efforts. There are comparatively few observers whose eyes have had such systematic training as to qualify them for work like this, and those who begin by expecting to see all that skilled observers see with an instrument of the same power are only laying up for themselves stores of disappointment. Mr. Mee's frank confession may be commended to the notice of those who hope to see at the first glance all that old students have learned to see by years of hard work. 'The first time I saw Saturn through a large telescope, a fine 12-inch reflector, I confess I could not see the division (Cassini's), though the view of the planet was one of exquisite beauty and long to be remembered, and notwithstanding the fact that the much fainter division of Encke was at the moment visible to the owner of the instrument!' It is extremely unlikely that the beginner will see the division with anything much less than 3 inches, and even with that aperture he will not see it until the rings are well opened. The writer's experience is that it is not by any means so readily seen as is sometimes supposed. Three inches will show it under good conditions; with 3⅞ it can be steadily held, even when the rings are only moderately open (steady holding is a very different thing from 'glimpsing'), but even with larger apertures the division becomes by no means a simple object as the rings close up (Fig. 26). In fact, there is nothing better fitted to fill the modern observer's mind with a most wholesome respect for the memory of a man like Cassini, than the thought that with his most imperfect appliances this great observer detected the division, a much more difficult feat than the mere seeing it when its existence and position are already known, and discovered also four of the Saturnian satellites. As for the minor divisions in the ring, if they are divisions, they are out of the question altogether for small apertures, and are often invisible even to skilled observers using the finest telescopes. Barnard's drawing (Plate XXIV.), as already noted, shows no trace of Encke's division; but nine months later the same observer saw it faintly in both ansæ of the ring. The conclusion from this and many similar observations seems to be that the marking is variable, as may very well be, from the constitution of the ring. The Crape Ring is beyond any instrument of less than four inches, and even with such an aperture requires favourable circumstances.

FIG. 26.

SATURN, 3⅞-inch.

With regard to a great number of very remarkable details which of late years have been seen and drawn by various observers, it may be remarked that the student need not be unduly disappointed should his small instrument fail, as it almost certainly will, to show these. This is a defect which his telescope shares with an instrument of such respectable size and undoubted optical quality as the Lick 36-inch. Writing in January, 1895, concerning the beautiful drawing which accompanies this chapter, Professor Barnard somewhat caustically observes: 'The black and white spots lately seen upon Saturn by various little telescopes were totally beyond the reach of the 36-inch—as well as of the 12-inch—under either good or bad conditions of seeing.... The inner edge (of the Crape Ring) was a uniform curve; the serrated or saw-toothed appearance of its inner edge which had previously been seen with some small telescopes was also beyond the reach of the 36-inch.' Such remarks should be consoling to those who find themselves and their instruments unequal to the remarkable feats which are sometimes accomplished, or recorded.

So far as one's personal experience goes, Saturn is generally the most easily defined of all the planets. Of late years he has been very badly placed for observers in the Northern Hemisphere, and this has considerably interfered with definition. But when well placed the planet presents a sharpness and steadiness of outline which render him capable of bearing higher magnifying powers than Jupiter, and even than Mars, though a curious rippling movement will often be noticed passing along the rings. It can scarcely be said, however, that there is much work for small instruments upon Saturn—the seeing of imaginary details being excluded. Accordingly, in spite of the undoubted beauty of the ringed planet, Jupiter will on the whole be found to be an object of more permanent interest. Yet, viewed merely as a spectacle, and as an example of extraordinary grace and symmetry, Saturn must always command attention. The sight of his wonderful system can hardly fail to excite speculation as to its destiny; and the question of the permanence of the rings is one that is almost thrust upon the spectator. With regard to this matter it may be noted that, according to Professor G. H. Darwin, the rings represent merely a passing stage in the evolution of the Saturnian system. At present they are within the limit proved by Roche, in 1848, to be that within which no secondary body of reasonable size could exist; and thus the discrete character of their constituents is maintained by the strains of unequal attraction. Professor Darwin believes that in time the inner particles of the ring will be drawn inwards, and will eventually fall upon the planet's surface, while the outer ones will disperse outwards to a point beyond Roche's limit, where they may eventually coalesce into a satellite or satellites—a poor compensation for the loss of appendages so brilliant and unique as the rings.

Saturn's train of satellites is the most numerous and remarkable in our system. As already mentioned, Huygens, the discoverer of the true form of the ring, discovered also the first and brightest satellite, Titan, which is a body somewhat larger than our own moon, having a diameter of 2,720 miles. A few years later came Cassini's discoveries of four other satellites, beginning in 1671 and ending in 1684. For more than 100 years discovery paused there, and it was not until August and September, 1789, that Sir William Herschel added the sixth and seventh to our knowledge of the Saturnian system.

In 1848 Bond in America and Lassell in England made independently the discovery of the eighth satellite—another of the coincidences which marked the progress of research upon Saturn, and in both of which Bond was concerned. Then followed another pause of fifty years broken by the discovery, in 1898, by Professor Pickering, of a ninth, whose existence was not completely confirmed till 1904. The motion of this satellite has proved to be retrograde, unlike that of the earlier discovered members of the family, so that its discovery has introduced us to a new and abnormal feature of the Saturnian system. The discoverer of Phœbe, as the ninth satellite has been named, has followed up his success by the discovery of a tenth member of Saturn's retinue, known provisionally as Themis. Accordingly the system, as at present known, consists of a triple ring and ten satellites. The last discovered moons are very small bodies, the diameter of Phœbe, for instance, being estimated at 150 miles; while its distance from Saturn is 8,000,000 miles. From the surface of the planet Phœbe would appear like a star of fifth or sixth magnitude; to observers on our own earth its magnitude is fifteenth or sixteenth. The ten satellites have been named as follows: 1, Titan, discovered by Huygens; 2, Japetus; 3, Rhea; 4, Dione; 5, Tethys, all discovered by Cassini; 6, Enceladus; and 7, Mimas, Sir William Herschel; 8, Hyperion, Bond and Lassell; 9, Phœbe; and 10, Themis, W. H. Pickering. Titan, the largest satellite, has been found to be considerably denser than Saturn himself.

The most of these little moons are, of course, beyond the power of small glasses; but a 2-inch will show Titan perfectly well. Japetus also is not a difficult object, but is much easier at his western than at his eastern elongation, a fact which probably points to a surface of unequal reflective power. Rhea, Dione, and Tethys are much more difficult. Kitchiner states that a friend of his saw them with $2\frac{7}{10}$-inch aperture, the planet being hidden; but probably his friend had been amusing himself at the quaint old gentleman's expense. Noble concludes that with a first-class 3-inch and under favourable circumstances four, or as a bare possibility even five, satellites may be seen; and I have repeatedly seen all the five with $3\frac{7}{8}$-inches. The only particular advantages of seeing them are the test which they afford of the instrument used, and the accompanying practice of the eye in picking up minute points of light. There is a considerable interest in watching the gradual disappearance of the brilliant disc of Saturn behind the edge of the field, or of the thick wire which may be placed in the eye-piece to hide the planet, and then catching the sudden flash up of the tiny dots of light which were previously lost in the glare of the larger body. For purposes of identification, recourse must be had to the 'Companion to the Observatory,' which prints lists of the elongations of the various satellites and a diagram of their orbits which renders it an easy matter to identify any particular satellite seen. Transits are, with the exception of that of Titan, beyond the powers of such instruments as we are contemplating. The shadow of Titan has, however, been seen in transit with a telescope of only 2⅞-inch aperture.

*The plane of the rings passes through the earth on April 13, and through the sun on July 27, 1907, at which periods it is probable that the rings will altogether disappear.

# CHAPTER XII

## URANUS AND NEPTUNE

Hitherto we have been dealing with bodies which, from time immemorial, have been known to man as planets. There must have been a period when one by one the various members of our system known to the ancients were discriminated from the fixed stars by unknown but patient and skilful observers; but, from the dawn of historical astronomy, up to the night of March 13, 1781, there had been no addition to the number of those five primary planets the story of whose discovery is lost in the mists of antiquity.

It may be questioned whether any one man, Kepler and Newton being possible exceptions, has ever done so much for the science of astronomy as was accomplished by Sir William Herschel. Certainly no single observer has ever done so much, or, which is almost more important than the actual amount of his achievement, has so completely revolutionized methods and ideas in observing.

A Hanoverian by birth, and a member of the band of the Hanoverian Guards, Herschel, after tasting the discomforts of war in the shape of a night spent in a ditch on the field of Hastenbeck, where that egregious general the Duke of Cumberland was beaten by the French, concluded that he was not designed by Nature for martial distinction, and abruptly solved the problem of his immediate destiny by recourse to the simple and unheroic expedient of desertion. He came to England, got employment after a time as organist of the Octagon Chapel at Bath, and was rapidly rising into notice as a musician, when the force of his genius, combined with a discovery which came certainly unsought, but was grasped as only a great man can grasp the gifts of Fortune, again changed the direction of his life, and gave him to the science of astronomy.

He had for several years employed his spare time in assiduous observation; and, finding that opticians' prices were higher than he could well afford, had begun to make Newtonian reflectors for himself, and had finally succeeded in constructing one of 6½ inches aperture, and of high optical quality. With this instrument, on the night of March 13, 1781, he was engaged in the execution of a plan which he had formed of searching the heavens for double stars, with a view to measuring their distance from the earth by seeing whether the apparent distance of the members of the double from one another varied in any degree in the course of the earth's journey round the sun. He was working through the stars in the constellation Gemini, when his attention was fixed by one which presented a different appearance from the others which had passed his scrutiny.

In a good telescope a fixed star shows only a very small disc, which indeed should be but a point of light; and the finer the instrument the smaller the disc. The disc of this object, however, was unmistakably larger than those of the fixed stars in its neighbourhood—unmistakably, that is, to an observer of such skill as Herschel, though those who have seen Uranus under ordinary powers will find their respect considerably increased for the skill which at once discriminated the tiny greenish disc from that of a fixed star. Subsequent observation revealed to Herschel that he was right in supposing that this body was not a star, for it proved to be in motion relatively to the stars among which it was seen. But, in spite of poetic authority, astronomical discoveries do not happen quite so dramatically as the sonnet 'On First looking into Chapman's Homer' suggests.

'Then felt I like some watcher of the skies,

When a new planet swims into his ken'

is a noble simile, were it only true to the facts. But new planets do not swim around promiscuously in this fashion; and in the case of Uranus, which more nearly realizes the thought of Keats than any other in the history of astronomy, the 'watcher of the skies' felt probably more puzzlement than anything else. Herschel was far from realizing that he had found a new planet. When unmistakable evidence was forthcoming that the newly discovered body was not a fixed star, he merely felt confirmed in the first conjecture which had been suggested by the size of its disc—namely, that he had discovered a new comet; and it was as a new comet that Uranus was first announced to the astronomical world.

It quickly became evident, however, that the new discovery moved in no cometary orbit, but in one which marked it out as a regular member of the solar system. A search was then instituted for earlier observations of the planet, and it was found to have been observed and mistaken for a fixed star on twenty previous occasions! One astronomer, Lemonnier, had actually observed it no fewer than twelve times, several of them within a few weeks of one another, and, had he but reduced and compared his observations, could scarcely have failed to have anticipated Herschel's discovery. But perhaps an astronomer who, like Lemonnier, noted some of his observations on a paper-bag which had formerly contained hair-powder, and whose astronomical papers have been described as 'the image of Chaos,' scarcely deserved the honour of such a discovery!

When it became known that this new addition to our knowledge of the solar system had been made by the self-taught astronomer at Bath, Herschel was summoned to Court by George III., and enabled to devote himself entirely to his favourite study by the bestowal of the not very magnificent pension of £200 a year, probably the best investment that has ever been made in the interests of astronomical science. In gratitude to the penurious monarch who had bestowed on him this meagre competence, Herschel wished to call his planet the Georgium Sidus—the Georgian Star, and this title, shortened in some instances to the Georgian, is still to be found in some ancient volumes on astronomy. The astronomers of the Continent, however, did not feel in the least inclined to elevate Farmer George to the skies before his due time, and for awhile the name of Herschel was given to the new planet, which still bears as its symbol the first letter of its discoverer's name with a globe attached to the cross-bar ♅ Finally, the name Urănus ('a' short) prevailed, and has for long been in universal use.

Uranus revolves round the sun at a distance from him of about 1,780,000,000 miles, in an orbit which takes eighty-four of our years to complete. Barnard gives his diameter at 34,900 miles, and if this measure be correct, he is the third largest planet of the system. Other measures give a somewhat smaller diameter, and place Neptune above him in point of size.

Subsequent observers have been able to see but little more than Herschel saw upon the diminutive disc to which even so large a body is reduced at so vast a distance. When near opposition, Uranus can readily be seen with the naked eye as a star of about the sixth magnitude, and there is no difficulty in picking him up with the finder of an ordinary telescope by means of an almanac and a good star map, nor in raising a small disc by the application of a moderately high power, say 200 and upwards. (Herschel was using 227 at the time of his discovery.) But small telescopes do little more than give their owners the satisfaction of seeing, pretty much as Herschel saw it, the object on which his eye was the first to light. Nor have even the largest instruments done very much more. Rings, similar to those of Saturn, were once suspected, but have long since been disposed of, and most of the observations of spots and belts have been gravely questioned. The Lick observers in 1890 and 1891 describe the belts as 'the merest shades on the planet's surface.'

The spectrum of Uranus is marked by peculiarities which distinguish it from that of the other planets. It is crossed by six dark absorption-bands, which indicate at all events that the medium through which the sunlight which it reflects to us has passed is of a constitution markedly different from that of our own atmosphere. It was at first thought that the spectrum gave evidence of the planet's self-luminosity; but this has not proved to be the case, though doubtless Uranus, like Jupiter and Saturn, is in the condition of a semi-sun. Like the other members of the group of large exterior planets, his density is small, being only ⅕ greater than that of water.

Six years after his great discovery, Herschel, with the 40-foot telescope of 4 feet in aperture which he had now built, discovered two satellites, and believed himself to have discovered four more. Later observations have shown that, in the case of the four, small stars near the planet had been mistaken for satellites. Subsequently two more were discovered, one by Lassell, and one by Otto Struve, making the number of the Uranian retinue up to four, so far as our present knowledge goes. These four satellites, known as Ariel, Umbriel, Oberon, and Titania, are distinguished by the fact that their orbits are almost perpendicular to the plane of the orbit of Uranus, and that the motions of all of them are retrograde. Titania and Oberon, the two discovered by Herschel, are the easiest objects; but although they are said to have been seen with a 4·3-inch refractor, this is a feat which no ordinary observer need hope to emulate. An 8-inch is a more likely instrument for such a task, and a 12-inch more likely still; the average observer will probably find the latter none too big. Accordingly, they are quite beyond the range of such observation as we are contemplating. The rotation period of Uranus is not known.

In a few years after the discovery of Uranus, it became apparent that by no possible ingenuity could his places as determined by present observation be satisfactorily combined with those determined by the twenty observations available, as already mentioned, from the period before he was recognised as a planet. Either the old observations were bad, or else the new planet was wandering from the track which it had formerly followed. It appeared to Bouvard, who was constructing the tables for the motions of Uranus, the simplest course to reject the old observations as probably erroneous, and to confine himself to the modern ones. Accordingly this course was pursued, and his tables were published in 1821, but only for it to be found that in a few years they also began to prove unsatisfactory; discrepancies began to appear and to increase, and it quickly became apparent that an attempt must be made to discover the cause of them.

Bouvard himself appears to have believed in the existence of a planet exterior to Uranus whose attraction was producing these disturbances, but he died in 1843 before any progress had been made with the solution of the enigma. In 1834 Hussey approached Airy, the Astronomer Royal, with the suggestion that he might sweep for the supposed exterior planet if some mathematician would help him as to the most likely region to investigate. Airy, however, returned a sufficiently discouraging answer, and Hussey apparently was deterred by it from carrying out a search which might very possibly have been rewarded by success. Bessel, the great German mathematician, had marked the problem for his own, and would doubtless have succeeded in solving it, but shortly after he had begun the gathering of material for his researches, he was seized with the illness which ultimately proved fatal to him.

The question was thus practically untouched when in 1841, John Couch Adams, then an undergraduate of St. John's College, Cambridge, jotted down a memorandum in which he indicated his resolve to attack it and attempt the discovery of the perturbing planet, 'as soon as possible after taking my degree.' The half-sheet of notepaper on which the memorandum was made is still extant, and forms part of the volume of manuscripts on the subject preserved in the library of St. John's College.

On October 21, 1845, Adams, who had taken his degree (Senior Wrangler) in 1843, communicated to Airy the results of his sixth and final attempt at the solution of the problem, and furnished him with the elements and mass of the perturbing planet, and an indication of its approximate place in the heavens. Airy, whose record in the matter reads very strangely, was little more inclined to give encouragement to Adams than to Hussey. He replied by propounding to the young investigator a question which he considered 'a question of vast importance, an *experimentum crucis*,' which Adams seemingly considered of so little moment, that strangely enough he never troubled to answer it. Then the matter dropped out of sight, though, had the planet been sought for when Adams's results were first communicated to the Astronomer Royal, it would have been found within 3½ lunar diameters of the place assigned to it.

Meanwhile, in France, another and better-known mathematician had taken up the subject, and in three memoirs presented to the French Academy of Sciences in 1846, Leverrier furnished data concerning the new planet which agreed in very remarkable fashion with those furnished by Adams to Airy. The coincidence shook Airy's scepticism, and he asked Dr. Challis, director of the Cambridge Observatory, to begin a search for the planet with the large Northumberland equatorial. Challis, who had no complete charts of the region to be searched, began to make observations for the construction of a chart which would enable him to detect the planet by means of its motion. It is more than likely that had he adopted Hussey's suggestion of simply sweeping in the vicinity of the spot indicated, he would have been successful, for the Northumberland telescope was of 11 inches aperture, and would have borne powers sufficient to distinguish readily the disc of Neptune from the fixed stars around it. However, Challis chose the more thorough, but longer method of charting; and even to that he did not devote undivided attention. 'Some wretched comet,' says Proctor, 'which he thought it his more important duty to watch, prevented him from making the reductions which would have shown him that the exterior planet had twice been recorded in his notes of observations.'

Indeed, a certain fatality seems to have hung over the attempts made in Britain to realize Adams's discovery. In 1845, the Rev. W. R. Dawes, one of the keenest and most skilful of amateur observers, was so much impressed by some of Adams's letters to the Astronomer Royal that he wrote to Lassell, asking him to search for the planet. When Dawes's letter arrived, Lassell was suffering from a sprained ankle, and laid the letter aside till he should be able to resume work. In the meantime the letter was burned by an officious servant-maid, and Lassell lost the opportunity of a discovery which would have crowned the fine work which he accomplished as an amateur observer.

A very different fate had attended Leverrier's calculations. On September 23, 1846, a letter from Leverrier was received at the Berlin Observatory, asking that search should be made for the planet in the position which his inquiries had pointed out. The same night Galle made the search, and within a degree of the spot indicated an object was found with a measurable disc of between two and three seconds diameter. As it was not laid down on Bremiker's star-chart of the region, it was clearly not a star, and by next night its planetary nature was made manifest. The promptitude with which Leverrier's results were acted upon by Encke and Galle is in strong contrast to the sluggishness which characterized the British official astronomers, who, indeed, can scarcely be said to have come out of the business with much credit.

A somewhat undignified controversy ensued. The French astronomers, very naturally, were eager to claim all the laurels for their brilliant countryman, and were indignant when a claim was put in on behalf of a young Englishman whose name had never previously been heard of. Airy, however, displayed more vigour in this petty squabble than in the search for Neptune, and presented such evidence in support of his fellow-countryman's right to recognition that it was impossible to deny him the honour which, but for official slackness, would have fallen to him as the actual as well as the potential discoverer of the new planet. Adams himself took no part in the strife; spoke, indeed, no words on the matter, except to praise the abilities of Leverrier, and gave no sign of the annoyance which most men in like circumstances would have displayed.

Galle suggested that the new planet should be called Janus; but the name of the two-faced god was felt to be rather too pointedly suitable at the moment, and that of Neptune was finally preferred. Neptune is about 32,900 miles in diameter, his distance from the sun is 2,792,000,000 miles, and he occupies

165 years in the circuit of his gigantic orbit. The spectroscopic evidence, such as it is, seems to point to a condition somewhat similar to that of Uranus.

Neptune had only been discovered seventeen days when Lassell found him to be attended by one satellite. First seen on October 10, 1846, it was not till the following July that the existence of this body was verified by Lassell himself and also by Otto Struve and Bond of Harvard. From the fact that it is visible at such an enormous distance, it is evident that this satellite must be of considerable size—probably at least equal to our own moon.

Small instruments can make nothing of Neptune beyond, perhaps, distinguishing the fact that, whatever the tiny disc may be, it is not that of a star. His satellite is an object reserved for the very finest instruments alone.

Should Neptune have any inhabitants, their sky must be somewhat barren of planets. Jupiter's greatest elongation from the sun would be about 10°, and he would be seen under somewhat less favourable conditions than those under which we see Mercury; while the planets between Jupiter and the sun would be perpetually invisible. Saturn and Uranus, however, would be fairly conspicuous, the latter being better seen than from the earth.

Suspicions have been entertained of the existence of another planet beyond Neptune, and photographic searches have been made, but hitherto without success. So far as our present knowledge goes, Neptune is the utmost sentinel of the regular army of the solar system.

# CHAPTER XIII

## COMETS AND METEORS

There is one type of celestial object which seldom fails to stir up the mind of even the most sluggishly unastronomical member of the community and to inspire him with an interest in the science—an interest which is usually conspicuous for a picturesque inaccuracy in the details which it accumulates, for a pathetic faith in the most extraordinary fibs which may be told in the name of science, and for a subsidence which is as rapid as the changes in the object which gave the inspiration. The sun may go on shining, a perpetual mystery and miracle, without attracting any attention, save when a wet spring brings on the usual talk of sun-spots and the weather; Jupiter and Venus excite only sufficient interest to suggest an occasional question as to whether that bright star is the Star of Bethlehem; but when a great comet spreads its fiery tail across the skies everybody turns astronomer for the nonce, and normally slumber-loving people are found willing, or at least able, to desert their beds at the most unholy hours to catch a glimpse of the strange and mysterious visitant. And, when the comet eventually withdraws from view again, as much inaccurate information has been disseminated among the public as would fill an encyclopædia, and require another to correct.

Comets are, however, really among the most interesting of celestial objects. Though we no longer imagine them to foretell wars, famines, and plagues, or complacently to indicate the approbation of heaven upon some illustrious person deceased or about to decease, and have almost ceased to shiver at the possibilities of a collision between a comet and the earth, they have within the last half century taken on a new and growing interest of a more legitimate kind, and there are few departments of science in which the advance of knowledge has been more rapid or which promise more in the immediate future, given material to work upon.

The popular idea of a comet is that it is a kind of bright wandering star with a long tail. Indeed, the star part of the conception is quite subsidiary to the tail part. The tail is *the* thing, and a comet without a tail is not worthy of attention, if it is not rather guilty of claiming notice on false pretences. As a matter of fact, the tail is absent in many comets and quite inconspicuous in many more; and a comet may be a body with any degree of resemblance or want of resemblance to the popular idea, from the faint globular stain of haze, scarcely perceptible in the telescopic field against the dark background of the sky, up to a magnificent object, which, like the dragon in the Revelation, seems to draw the third part of the stars of heaven after it—an object like the Donati comet of 1858, with a nucleus brighter than a first-magnitude star, and a tail like a great feathery plume of light fifty millions of miles in length. It seems as impossible to set limits to the variety of form of which comets are capable as it is to set limits to their number.

Generally speaking, however, a comet consists of three parts: The nucleus—which appears as a more or less clearly defined star-like point, and is the only part of the comet which will bear any magnification to speak of—the coma, and the tail. In many telescopic comets the nucleus is entirely absent, and, in the comets in which it is present, it is of very varied size, and often presents curious irregularities in shape, and even occasionally the appearance of internal motions. It frequently changes very much in size during the period of the comet's visibility. The nucleus is the only part of a comet's structure which has even the most distant claim to solidity; but even so the evidence which has been gradually accumulated all goes to show that while it may be solid in the sense of being composed of particles which have some substance, it is not solid in the sense of being one coherent mass, but rather consists of something like a swarm of small meteoric bodies. Surrounding the nucleus is the coma, from which the comet derives its name. This is a sort of misty cloud through which the nucleus seems to shine like a star in a nebula or a gas-lamp in a fog. Its boundaries are difficult to trace, as it appears to fade away gradually on every side into the background; but generally its appearance is more or less of a globular shape except where the tail streams away from it behind. Sometimes the coma is of enormous extent—the Great Comet of 1811 showed a nucleus of 428 miles diameter, enclosed within a nebulous globe 127,000 miles across, which in its turn was wrapped in a luminous atmosphere of four times greater diameter, with an outside envelope covering all, and extending backwards to form the tail. But it is also of the most extraordinary tenuity, the light of the very faintest stars having been frequently observed to shine undimmed through several millions of miles of coma. Finally, there is the tail, which may be so short as to be barely distinguishable; or may extend, as in the case of Comet 1811 (ii.), to 130,000,000 miles; or, as in that of Comet 1843 (i.), to 200,000,000. The most tenuous substances with which we are acquainted seem to be solidity itself compared with the material of a comet's tail. It is 'such stuff as dreams are made of.'

Comets fall into two classes. There are those whose orbits follow curves that are not closed, like the circle or the ellipse, but appear to extend indefinitely into space. A comet following such an orbit (parabolic or hyperbolic) seems to come wandering in from the depths of space, passes round the sun, and then gradually recedes into the space from which it came, never again to be seen of human eye. It is now becoming questionable, however, whether any comet can really be said to come in from infinite space; and the view is being more generally held that orbits which to us appear portions of unclosed curves may in reality be only portions of immensely elongated ellipses, and that all comets are really members of the solar system, travelling away, indeed, to distances that are immense compared with even the largest planetary orbit, but yet infinitely small compared with the distances of the fixed stars.

Second, there are those comets whose orbits form ellipses with a greater or less departure from the circular form. Such comets must always return again, sooner or later, to the neighbourhood of the sun, which occupies one of the foci of the ellipse, and they are known as Periodic Comets. The orbits which they follow may have any degree of departure from the circular form, from one which does not differ very notably from that of such a planet as Eros, up to one which may be scarcely distinguishable from a parabola. Thus we have Periodic Comets again divided into comets of short and comets of long period. In the former class, the period ranges from that of Encke's comet which never travels beyond the orbit of Jupiter, and only takes 3·29 years to complete its journey, up to that of the famous comet whose periodicity was first discovered by Halley, whose extreme distance from the sun is upwards of 3,200,000,000 miles, and whose period is 76·78 years. Comets of long period range from bodies which only require a paltry two or three centuries to complete their revolution, up to others whose journey has to be timed by thousands of years. In the case of these latter bodies, there is scarcely any distinction to be made between them and those comets which are not supposed to be periodic; the ellipse of a comet which takes three or four thousand years to complete its orbit is scarcely to be distinguished, in the small portion of it that can be traced, from a parabola.

Several comets have been found to be short period bodies, which, though bright enough to have been easily seen, have yet never been noticed at any previous appearance. It is known that some at least of these owe their present orbits to the fact that having come near to one or other of the planets they have been, so to speak, captured, and diverted from the track which they formerly pursued. Several of the planets have more or less numerous flocks of comets associated with them which they have thus captured and introduced into a short period career. Jupiter has more than a score in his group, while Saturn, Uranus and Neptune have smaller retinues. There can be no question that a comet of first-class splendour, such as that of 1811, that of 1858, or that of 1861, is one of the most impressive spectacles that the heavens have to offer. Unfortunately it is one which the present generation, at least in the northern hemisphere, has had but little opportunity of witnessing. Chambers notices 'that it may be taken as a fact that a bright and conspicuous comet comes about once in ten years, and a very remarkable comet once every thirty years;' and adds, 'tested then by either standard of words "bright and conspicuous," or "specially celebrated," it may be affirmed that a good comet is now due.' It is eleven years since that hopeful anticipation was penned, and we are still waiting, not only for the 'specially celebrated,' but even for the 'bright and conspicuous' comet; so that on the whole we may be said to have a grievance. Still, there is no saying when the grievance may be removed, as comets have a knack of being unexpected in their developments; and it may be that some unconsidered little patch of haze is even now drawing in from the depths which may yet develop into a portent as wonderful as those that astonished the generation before us in 1858 and 1861.

The multitude of comets is, in all probability, enormous. Between the beginning of the Christian era and 1888 the number recorded was, according to Chambers, 850; but the real number for that period must have been indefinitely greater, as, for upwards of 1600 out of the 1888 years, only those comets which were visible to the naked eye could have been recorded—a very small proportion of the whole. The period 1801 to 1888 shows 270, so that in less than one century there has been recorded almost one-third of the total for nineteen centuries. At present no year goes by without the discovery of several comets; but very few of them become at all conspicuous. For example, in 1904, six comets were seen—three of these being returns of comets previously observed, and three new discoveries; but none of these proved at all notable objects in the ordinary sense, though Comet 1904 (*a*), discovered by Brooks, was pretty generally observed.

It would serve no useful purpose to repeat here the stories of any of the great comets. These may be found in considerable detail in such volumes as Chambers's 'Handbook of Astronomy,' vol. i., or Miss Agnes Clerke's 'History of Astronomy.' Attention must rather be turned to the question, 'What are comets?' It is a question to which no answer of a satisfactory character could be given till within the last fifty years. Even the great comet of 1858, the Donati, which made so deep an impression on the public mind, and was so closely followed and studied by astronomers, was not the medium of any great advance in the knowledge of cometary nature. The many memoirs which it elicited disclosed nothing fundamentally new, and broke out no new lines of inquiry. Two things have since then revolutionized the study of the subject—the application of the spectroscope to the various comets that have appeared in the closing years of the nineteenth century, and the discovery of the intimate connection between comets and meteors.

It was in 1864, a year further made memorable astronomically by Sir William Huggins's discovery of the gaseous nature of some of the nebulæ, that the spectroscope was first applied to the study of a comet. The celestial visitor thus put to the question, a comet discovered by Tempel, was in nowise a distinguished object, appearing like a star of the second magnitude, or less, with a feeble though fairly long tail. When analyzed by Donati, it was found to yield a spectrum consisting of three bright bands, yellow, green, and blue, separated by dark spaces. This observation at once modified ideas as to cometary structure. Hitherto it had been supposed that comets shone by reflected light; but Donati's observation revealed beyond question that the light of the 1864 comet at all events was inherent, and that, so far as the observation went, the comet consisted of glowing gas.

**PLATE XXV.**

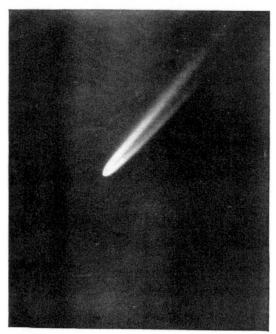

Great Comet. Photographed May 5, 1901, with the 13-inch Astrographic Refractor of the Royal Observatory, Cape of Good Hope.

In 1868 Sir William Huggins carried the matter one step further by showing that the spectrum of Winnecke's comet of that year agreed with that of olefiant gas rendered luminous by electricity; and the presence of the hydrocarbon spectrum has since been detected in a large number of comets. The first really brilliant comet to be analyzed by the spectroscope was

Coggia's (1874), and it presented not only the three bright bands that had been already seen, but the whole range of five bands characteristic of the hydrocarbon spectrum. In certain cases, however—notably, that of Holmes's comet of 1892 and that of the great southern comet of 1901 (Plate XXV.)—the spectrum has not exhibited the usual bright band type, but has instead shown merely a continuous ribbon of colour. From these analyses certain facts emerge. First, that the gaseous surroundings of comets consist mainly of hydrogen and carbon, and that in all probability their luminosity is due, not to mere solar heat, but to the effect of some electric process acting upon them during their approach to the sun; and second, that, along with these indications of the presence of luminous hydrocarbon compounds, there is also evidence of the existence of solid particles, mainly in the nucleus, but also to some extent in the rest of the comet, which shine by reflected sunlight. It is further almost certain, from the observation by Elkin and Finlay of the beginning of the transit of Comet 1882 (iii.) across the sun's face, that this solid matter is not in any sense a solid mass. The comet referred to disappeared absolutely as soon as it began to pass the sun's edge. Had it been a solid mass or even a closely compacted collection of small bodies it would have appeared as a black spot upon the solar surface. The conclusion, then, is obvious that the solid matter must be very thinly and widely spread, while its individual particles may have any size from that of grains of sand up to that of the large meteoric bodies which sometimes reach our earth.

Thus the state of the case as regards the constitution of comets is, roughly speaking, this: They consist of a nucleus of solid matter, held together, but with a very slack bond, by the power of gravitation. From this nucleus, as the comet approaches perihelion, the electric action of the sun, working in a manner at present unknown, drives off volumes of luminous gas, which form the tail; and in some comets the waves of this vapour have been actually seen rising slowly in successive pulses from the nucleus, and then being driven backwards much as the smoke of a steamer is driven. It has been found also by investigation of Comet Wells 1882 and the Great Comet of 1882 that in some at least of these bodies sodium and iron are present.

The question next arises, What becomes of comets in the end? Kepler long ago asserted his belief that they perished, as silkworms perish by spinning their own thread, exhausting themselves by the very efforts of tail-production which render them sometimes so brilliant to observation; and this seems to be pretty much the case. Thus Halley's comet, which was once so brilliant and excited so much attention, was at its last visit a very inconspicuous object indeed. At its apparition in 1845-1846 Biela's comet was found to have split into two separate bodies, which were found at their return in 1852 to have parted company widely. Since that year it has never been observed again in the form of a comet, though, as we shall see, it has presented itself in a different guise. The same fate has overtaken the comets of De Vico (1844), and Brorsen (1846). The former should have returned in 1850, but failed to keep its appointment; and the latter, after having established a character for regularity by returning to observation on four occasions, failed to appear in 1890, and has never since been seen.

The mystery of such disappearances has been at least partially dispelled by the discovery, due to Schiaparelli and other workers in the same field, that various prominent meteor-showers travel in orbits precisely the same as those of certain comets. Thus the shower of meteors which takes place with greater or less brilliancy every year from a point in the constellation Perseus has been proved to follow the orbit of the bright comet of 1862; while the great periodic shower of the Leonids follows the track of the comet of 1866; the orbit of the star-shower of April 20—the Lyrids—corresponds with that of a comet seen in 1861; and the disappearance of Biela's comet appears to be accounted for by the other November shower whose radiant point is in the constellation Andromeda. In fact, the state of the matter is well summed up by Kirkwood's question: 'May not our periodic meteors be the débris of ancient but now disintegrated comets, whose matter has become distributed round their orbits?' The loosely compacted mass which forms the nucleus of the comet appears to gradually lose its cohesion under the force of solar tidal action, and its fragments come to revolve independently in their orbit, for a time in a loosely gathered swarm, and then gradually, as the laggards drop behind, in the form of a complete ring of meteoric bodies, which are distributed over the whole orbit. The Leonid shower is in the first condition, or, rather, was when it was last seen, for it seems to be now lost to us; the Perseid shower is in the second. The shower of the Andromedes has since confirmed its identity with the lost comet of Biela by displays in 1872, 1885, and 1892, at the seasons when that comet should have returned to the neighbourhood of the sun. It appears to be experiencing the usual fate of such showers, and becoming more widely distributed round its orbit, and the return in 1905 was very disappointing, the reason apparently being that the dense group in close attendance on the comet has suffered disturbance from Jupiter and Saturn, and now passes more than a million miles outside the earth's orbit.

In 1843 there appeared one of the most remarkable of recorded comets. It was not only of conspicuous brilliancy and size, though its tail at one stage reached the enormous length of 200,000,000 miles, but was remarkable for the extraordinarily close approach which it made to the sun. Its centre came as near to the sun as 78,000 miles, leaving no more than 32,000 miles between the surfaces of the two bodies; it must, therefore, have passed clear through the corona, and very probably through some of the prominences. Its enormous tail was whirled, or rather appeared to be whirled, right round the sun in a little over two hours, thus affording conclusive proof that the tail of a comet cannot possibly be an appendage, but must consist of perpetually renewed emanations from the nucleus. But in addition to these wonders, the comet of 1843 proved the precursor of a series of fine comets travelling in orbits which were practically identical. The great southern comet of 1880 proved, when its orbit had been computed, to follow a path almost exactly the same as that of its predecessor of thirty-seven years before. It seemed inconceivable that a body so remarkable as the 1843 comet should have a period of only thirty-seven years, and yet never previously have attracted attention. Before the question had been fairly discussed, it was accentuated by the discovery, in 1881, of a comet whose orbit was almost indistinguishable from that of the comet of 1807. But the 1807 comet was not due to return till A.D. 3346. Further, the comet of 1881 proved to have a period, not of seventy-four years, as would have been the case had it been a return of that of 1807, but of 2,429 years. The only possible conclusion was that here were two comets which were really fragments of one great comet which had suffered disruption, as Biela's comet visibly did, and that one fragment followed in the other's wake with an interval of seventy-four years.

Meanwhile, the question of the 1843 and 1880 comets was still unsettled, and it received a fresh complication by the appearance of the remarkable comet of 1882, whose transit of the sun has been already alluded to, for the orbit of this new body proved to be a reproduction, almost, but not quite exact, of those of the previous two. Astronomers were at a greater loss than ever, for if this were a return of the 1880 comet, then the conclusion followed that something was so influencing its orbit as to have shortened its period from thirty-seven to two years. The idea of the existence of some medium round the sun, capable of resisting bodies which passed through it, and thus causing them to draw closer to their centre of attraction and shortening their periods, was now revived, and it seemed as though, at its next return, this wonderful visitant must make the final plunge into the photosphere, with what consequences none could foretell. These forebodings proved to be quite baseless. The comet passed so close to the sun (within 300,000 miles of his surface), that it must have been sensibly retarded at its passage by the resisting medium, had such a thing existed; but not the slightest retardation was discernible. The comet suffered no check in its plunge through the solar surroundings, and consequently the theory of the resisting medium may be said to have received its quietus.

Computation showed that the 1882 comet followed nearly the same orbit as its predecessors; and thus we are faced by the fact of families of comets, travelling in orbits that are practically identical, and succeeding one another at longer or shorter intervals. The idea that these families have each sprung from the disruption of some much larger body seems to be most probable, and it appears to be confirmed by the fact that in the 1882 comet the process of further disruption was actually witnessed. Schmidt of Athens detected one small offshoot of the great comet, which remained visible for several days. Barnard a few days later saw at least six small nebulous bodies close to their parent, and a little later Brooks observed another. 'Thus,' as Miss Agnes Clerke remarks, 'space appeared to be strewn with the filmy débris of this beautiful but fragile structure all along the track of its retreat from the sun.'

The state of our knowledge with regard to comets may be roughly summed up. We have extreme tenuity in the whole body, even the nucleus being apparently not solid, but a comparatively loose swarm of solid particles. The nucleus, in all likelihood, shines by reflected sunlight—in part, at all events. The nebulous surroundings and tail are produced by solar action upon the matter of which the comet is composed, this action being almost certainly electrical, though heat may play some part in it. The nebulous matter appears to proceed in waves from the nucleus, and to be swept backward along the comet's track by some repellent force, probably electrical, exerted by the sun. This part of the comet's structure consists mainly of self-luminous gases, generally of the hydrocarbon type, though sodium and iron have also been traced. Comets, certainly in many cases, probably in all, suffer gradual degradation into swarms of meteors. The existence of groups of comets, each group probably the outcome of the disruption of a much larger body, is demonstrated by the fact of successive comets travelling in almost identically similar orbits. Finally, comets are all connected with the solar system, so far, at least, that they accompany that system in its journey of 400,000,000 miles a year through space. Our system does not, as it were, pick up the comets as it sweeps along upon its great journey; it carries them along with it.

A few words may be added as to cometary observation. It is scarcely likely that any very great number of amateur observers will ever be attracted by the branch of comet-hunting. The work is somewhat monotonous and laborious, and seems to require special aptitudes, and, above all, an enormous endowment of patience. Probably the true comet-hunter, like the poet, is born, not made; and it is not likely that there are, nor desirable that there should be, many individuals of the type of Messier, the 'comet-ferret.' 'Messier,' writes a contemporary, 'is at all events a very good man, and simple as a child. He lost his wife some years ago, and his attendance upon her death-bed prevented his being the discoverer of a comet for which he had been lying in wait, and which was snatched from him by Montaigne de Limoges. This made him desperate. A visitor began to offer him consolation for his recent bereavement, when Messier, thinking only of the comet, answered, "I had discovered twelve; alas! to be robbed of the thirteenth by that Montaigne!" and his eyes filled with tears. Then, recollecting that it was necessary to deplore his wife, he exclaimed, "Ah! cette pauvre femme!" and again wept for his comet.' In addition to the fact that few have reached such a degree of scientific detachment as to put a higher value upon a comet than upon the nearest of relatives, there is the further fact that the future of cometary discovery, and of the record of cometary change seems to lie almost entirely with photography, which is wonderfully adapted for the work (Plate XXVI.).

**PLATE XXVI.**

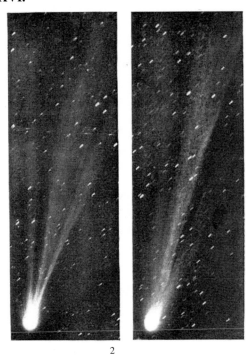

1                                        2

Photographs of Swift's Comet. By Professor E. E. Barnard.

1. Taken April 4, 1892; exposure 1 hour. 2. Taken April 6, 1892; exposure 1 hour 5 minutes.

Anyone who desires to become a comet-hunter must, in addition to the possession of the supreme requisites, patience and perseverance, provide himself with an instrument of at least 4 inches aperture, together with a good and comprehensive set of star-charts and the New General Catalogue of nebulæ with the additions which have been made to it. The reason for this latter item of equipment is the fact that many telescopic comets are scarcely to be distinguished from nebulæ, and that an accurate knowledge of the nebulous objects in the regions to be searched for comets, or at least a means of quickly identifying such objects, is therefore indispensable. The portions of the heavens which afford the most likely fields for discovery will naturally be those in the vicinity of where the sun has set at evening, or where he is about to rise in the early morning, all comets having of necessity to approach the sun more or less closely at their perihelion passage. Other parts of the heavens should not be neglected; but these are the most likely neighbourhoods.

Most of us, however, will be content to discover our comets in the columns of the daily newspaper, or by means of a post-card from some obliging friend. The intimation, in whatever way received, will generally contain the position of the comet at a certain date, given in right ascension and declination, and either a statement of its apparent daily motion, or else a provisional set of places for several days ahead. Having either of these, the comet's position must be marked down on the star-map, and the course which it is likely to pursue must be traced out in pencil by means of the data—a perfectly simple matter of marking down the position for each day by its celestial longitude and latitude as given. The observer will next note carefully the alignment of the comet with the most conspicuous stars in the neighbourhood of the particular position for the day of his observation; and, guiding his telescope by means of these, will point it as nearly as possible to that position. He may be lucky enough to hit upon his object at once, especially if it be a comparatively bright one. More probably, he will have to 'sweep' for it. In this case the telescope must be pointed some little distance below and to one side of the probable position of the comet, and moved slowly and gently along, careful watch being kept upon the objects which pass through the field, until a similar distance on the opposite side of the position has been reached. Then raise the instrument by not more than half a field's breadth, estimating this by the stars in the field, and repeat the process in the opposite direction, going on until the comet appears in the field, or until it is obvious that it has been missed. A low power should be used at first, which may be changed for a somewhat higher one when the object has been found. But in no case will the use of really high magnifiers be found advisable. It is, of course, simply impossible with the tail, for which the naked eye is the best instrument, nor can the coma bear any degree of magnification, though occasionally the nucleus may be sufficiently sharply defined to bear moderate powers. The structure of the latter should be carefully observed, with particular attention to the question of whether any change can be seen in it, or whether there seem any tendency to such a multiplication of nuclei as characterized the great comet of 1882. It is possible that the pulses of vapour sunwards from the nucleus may also be observed.

Appearance of motion, wavy or otherwise, in the tail, should also be looked for, and carefully watched if seen. Beyond this there is not very much that the ordinary observer can do; the determination of positions requires more elaborate appliances, and the spectroscope is necessary for any study of cometary constitution. It only remains to express a wish for the speedy advent of a worthy subject for operations.

We turn now to those bodies which, as has been pointed out, appear to be the débris of comets which have exhausted their cometary destiny, and ceased to have a corporate existence. Everyone is familiar with the phenomenon known as a meteor, or shooting-star, and there are few clear nights on which an observer who is much in the open will not see one or more of these bodies. Generally they become visible in the form of a bright point of light which traverses in a straight line a longer or shorter path across the heavens, and then vanishes, sometimes leaving behind it for a second or two a faintly luminous train. The shooting-stars are of all degrees of brightness, from the extremely faint streaks which sometimes flash across the field of the telescope, up to brilliant objects, brighter than any of the planets or fixed stars, and sometimes lighting up the whole landscape with a light like that of the full moon.

The prevailing opinion, down to a comparatively late date, was that shooting-stars were mere exhalations in the earth's atmosphere, arising as one author expressed it, 'from the fermentation of acid and alkaline bodies, which float in the atmosphere'; and it was also suggested by eminent astronomers that they were the products of terrestrial volcanoes, returning, after long wanderings, to their native home.

The true study of meteoric astronomy may be said to date from the year 1833, when a shower of most extraordinary splendour was witnessed. The magnificence of this display was the means of turning greater attention to the subject; and it was observed as a fact, though the importance of the observation was scarcely realized, that the meteors all appeared to come from nearly the one point in the constellation Leo. The fact of there being a single radiant point implied that the meteors were all moving in parallel lines, and had entered our atmosphere from a vast distance. Humboldt, who had witnessed a previous appearance of this shower in 1799, suggested that it might be a periodic phenomenon; and his suggestion was amply confirmed when in 1866 the shower made its appearance again in scarcely diminished splendour. Gradually other showers came to be recognised, and their radiant points fixed; and meteoric astronomy began to be established upon a scientific basis.

In 1866 Schiaparelli announced that the shower which radiates in August from the constellation Perseus follows the same track as that of Swift's comet (1862 iii.); and in the following year the great November shower from Leo, already alluded to, was proved to have a similar connection with Tempel's comet (1866 i.). The shower which comes from the constellation Lyra, about April 20, describes the same orbit as that of Comet 1861 i.; while, as already mentioned, the mysterious disappearance of Biela's comet received a reasonable explanation by its association with the other great November shower—that which radiates from the constellation Andromeda. With regard to the last-named shower, it has not only been shown that the meteors are associated with Biela's comet, but also that they separated from it subsequent to 1841, in which year the comet's orbit was modified by perturbations from Jupiter. The Andromeda meteors follow the modified orbit, and hence must have been in close association with the comet when the perturbation was exercised.

The four outstanding meteor radiants are those named, but there are very many others. Mr. Denning, to whom this branch of science owes so much, estimates the number of distinct radiants known at about 4,400; and it seems likely that every one of these showers, some of them, of course very feeble, represents some comet deceased. The history of a meteor shower would appear to be something like this: When the comet, whose executor it is, has but recently deceased, it will appear as a very brilliant periodic shower, occurring on only one or two nights exactly at the point where the comet in its journeying would have crossed the earth's track, and appearing only at the time when the comet itself would have been there. Gradually the meteors get more and more tailed out along the orbit, as runners of unequal staying powers get strung out over a track in a long race, until the displays may be repeated, with somewhat diminished splendour, year after year for several years before and after the time when the parent comet is due. At last they get thinly spread out over the whole orbit, and the shower becomes an annual one, happening each year when the earth crosses the orbit of the comet. This has already happened to the Perseid shower; at least 500,000,000 miles of the orbit of Biela's comet are studded with representatives of the Andromedes; and the Leonid shower had already begun to show symptoms of the same process at its appearance in 1866. Readers will remember the disappointment caused by the failure of the Leonid shower to come up to time in 1899, and it seems probable that the action of some perturbing cause has so altered the orbit of this shower that it now passes almost clear of the earth's path, so that we shall not have the opportunity of witnessing another great display of the Leonid meteors.

So far as is known, no member of one of these great showers has ever fallen to the earth. There are two possible exceptions to this statement, as in 1095 a meteor fell to the ground during the progress of a shower of Lyrids, and in 1885 another fell during a display of the Andromedes. In neither case, however, was the radiant point noted, and unless it was the same as that of the shower the fall of the meteor was a mere coincidence. It seems probable that this is the case, and the absence of any evidence that a specimen from a cometary shower has reached the earth points to the extreme smallness of the various members of the shower and also to the fine division of the matter of the original comet.

In addition to the meteors originating from systematic showers, there are also to be noted frequent and sometimes very brilliant single meteors. Specimens of these have in many instances been obtained. They fall into three classes —'Those in which iron is found in considerable amount are termed siderites; those containing an admixture of iron and stone, siderolites; and those consisting almost entirely of stone are known as aerolites' (Denning). The mass of some of these bodies is very considerable. Swords have been forged out of their iron, one of which is in the possession of President Diaz of Mexico, while diamonds have been found in meteoric irons which fell in Arizona. It may be interesting to know that, according to a grave decision of the American courts, a meteor is 'real estate,' and belongs to the person on whose ground it has fallen; the alternative—that it is 'wild game,' and the property of its captor—having been rejected by the court. So far as I am aware, the legal status of these interesting flying creatures has not yet been determined in Britain.

The department of meteoric astronomy is one in which useful work can be done with the minimum of appliances. The chief requisites are a good set of star-maps, a sound knowledge of the constellations, a straight wand, and, above all, patience. The student must make himself familiar with the constellations (a pleasant task, which should be part of everyone's education), so that when a meteor crosses his field of view he may be able to identify at once with an approach to accuracy its points of appearance and disappearance. It is here that the straight wand comes into play. Mr. Denning advises the use of it as a means of guiding the eye. It is held so as to coincide with the path of the meteor just seen, and will thus help the eye to estimate the position and slope of the track relatively to the stars of the constellations which it has crossed. This track should be marked as quickly as possible on the charts. Mere descriptions of the appearance of meteors, however beautiful, are quite valueless. It is very interesting to be told that a meteor when first seen was 'of the size and colour of an orange,' but later 'of the apparent size of the full moon, and surrounded by a mass of glowing vapour which further increased its size to that of the head of a flour-barrel'; but the description is scarcely marked by sufficient precision of statement for scientific purposes.

The observer must note certain definite points, of which the following is a summary: (1) Date, hour, and minute of appearance. (2) Brightness, compared with some well-known star, planet, or, if exceptionally bright, with the moon. (3) Right ascension and declination of point of first appearance. (4) The same of point of disappearance. (5) Length of track. (6) Duration of visibility. (7) Colour, presence of streak or train, and any other notable features. (8) Radiant point.

When these have been given with a reasonable approach to accuracy, the observer has done his best to provide a real, though small, contribution to the sum of human knowledge; nor is the determination of these points so difficult as would at first appear from their number. The fixing of the points of appearance and disappearance and of the radiant will present a little difficulty to start with; but in this, as in all other matters, practice will bring efficiency. It may be mentioned that the efforts of those who take up this subject would be greatly increased in usefulness by their establishing a connection with the Meteor Section of the British Astronomical Association.

One curious anomaly has been established by Mr. Denning's patient labour—the existence, namely, of what are termed 'stationary radiants.' It is obvious that if meteors have the cometary connection already indicated, their radiant point should never remain fixed; as the showers move onwards in their orbit they should leave the original radiant behind. Mr. Denning has conclusively proved, however, that there are showers which do not follow the rule in this respect, but proceed from a radiant which remains the same night after night, some feeble showers maintaining the same radiant for several months. It is not easy to see how this fact is to be reconciled with the theory of cometary origin; but the fact itself is undeniable.

# CHAPTER XIV

## THE STARRY HEAVENS

We now leave the bounds of our own system, and pass outwards towards the almost infinite spaces and multitudes of the fixed stars. In doing so we are at once confronted with a wealth and profusion of beauty and a vastness of scale which are almost overwhelming. Hitherto we have been dealing almost exclusively with bodies which, though sometimes considerably larger than our world, were yet, with the exception of the sun, of the same class and comparable with it; and with distances which, though very great indeed, were still not absolutely beyond the power of apprehension. But now all former scales and standards have to be left behind, for even the vast orbit of Neptune, 5,600,000,000 of miles in diameter, shrinks into a point when compared with the smallest of the stellar distances. Even our unit of measurement has to be changed, for miles, though counted in hundreds of millions, are inadequate; and, accordingly, the unit in which our distance from the stars is expressed is the 'light year,' or the distance travelled by a ray of light in a year.

Light travels at the rate of about 186,000 miles a second, and therefore leaps the great gulf between our earth and the sun in about eight minutes. But even the nearest of the fixed stars—Alpha Centauri, a star of the first magnitude in the Southern Hemisphere—is so incredibly distant that light takes four years and four months to travel to us from it; while the next nearest, a small star in Ursa Major, is about seven light-years distant, and the star 61 of the constellation Cygnus, the first northern star whose distance was measured, is separated from us by two years more still.

At present the distances of about 100 stars are known approximately; but it must be remembered that the approximation is a somewhat rough one. The late Mr. Cowper Ranyard once remarked of measures of star-distances that they would be considered rough by a cook who was in the habit of measuring her salt by the cupful and her pepper by the pinch. And the remark has some truth—not because of any carelessness in the measurements, for they are the results of the most minute and scrupulous work with the most refined instrumental means that modern skill can devise and construct—but because the quantities to be measured are almost infinitely small.

It is at present considered that the average distance from the earth of stars of the first magnitude is thirty-three light years, that of stars of the second fifty-two, and of the third eighty-two. In other words, when we look at such stars on any particular evening, we are seeing them, not as they are at the moment of observation, but as they were thirty-three, fifty-two, or eighty-two years ago, when the rays of light which render them visible to us started on their almost inconceivable journey. The fact of the average distance of first-magnitude stars being less than that of second, and that of second in turn less than that of third, is not to be held as implying that there are not comparatively small stars nearer to us than some very bright ones. Several insignificant stars are considerably nearer to us than some of the most brilliant objects in the heavens—*e.g.*, 61 Cygni, which is of magnitude 4·8, is almost infinitely nearer to us than the very brilliant first magnitude star Rigel in Orion. The rule holds only on the average.

The number of the stars is not less amazing than their distance. It is true that the number visible to the unaided eye is not by any means so great as might be imagined on a casual survey. On a clear night the eye receives the impression that the multitude of stars is so great as to be utterly beyond counting; but this is not the case. The naked-eye, or 'lucid,' stars have frequently been counted, and it has been found that the number visible to a good average eye in both hemispheres together is about 6,000. This would give for each hemisphere 3,000, and making allowance for those lost to sight in the denser air near the horizon, or invisible by reason of restricted horizon, it is probable that the number of stars visible at any one time to any single observer in either hemisphere does not exceed 2,500. In fact Pickering estimates the total number visible, down to and including the sixth magnitude, to be only 2,509 for the Northern Hemisphere, and on that basis it may safely be assumed that 2,000 would be the extreme limit for the average eye.

**PLATE XXVII.**

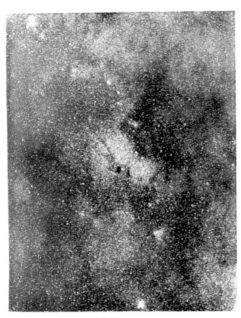

Region of the Milky Way in Sagittarius. Photographed by Professor E. E. Barnard.

But this somewhat disappointing result is more than atoned for when the telescope is called in and the true richness of the heavenly host begins to appear. Let us take for illustration a familiar group of stars—the Pleiades. The number of stars visible to an ordinary eye in this little group is six; keen-sighted people see eleven, or even fourteen. A small telescope converts the Pleiades into a brilliant array of luminous points to be counted not by units but by scores, while the plates taken with a modern photographic telescope of 13 inches aperture show 2,326 stars. The Pleiades, of course, are a somewhat notable group; but those who have seen any of the beautiful photographs of the heavens, now so common, will know that in many parts of the sky even this great increase in number is considerably exceeded; and that for every star the eye sees in such regions a moderate telescope will show 1,000, and a great instrument perhaps 10,000. It is extremely probable that the number of stars visible with the largest telescopes at present in use would not be overstated at 100,000,000 (Plate XXVII.).

It is evident, on the most casual glance at the sky, that in the words of Scripture, 'One star differeth from another star in glory.' There are stars of every degree of brilliancy, from the sparkling white lustre of Sirius or Vega, down to the dim glimmer of those stars which are just on the edge of visibility, and are blotted out by the faintest wisp of haze. Accordingly, the stars have been divided into 'magnitudes' in terms of scales which, though arbitrary, are yet found to be of general convenience. Stars of the first six magnitudes come under the title of 'lucid' stars; below the sixth we come to the telescopic stars, none of which are visible to the naked eye, and which range down to the very last degree of faintness. Of stars of the first magnitude there are recognised about twenty, more or less. By far the brightest star visible to us in the Northern Hemisphere, though it is really below the Equator, is Sirius, whose brightness exceeds by no fewer than fourteen and a half times that of Regulus, the twentieth star on the list. The next brightest stars, Canopus and Alpha Centauri, are also Southern stars, and are not visible to us in middle latitudes. The three brightest of our truly Northern stars, Vega, Capella, and Arcturus, come immediately after Alpha Centauri, and opinions are much divided as to their relative brightness, their diversity in colour and in situation rendering a comparison somewhat difficult. The other conspicuous stars of the first magnitude visible in our latitudes are, in order of brightness, Rigel, Procyon, Altair, Betelgeux, Aldebaran, Pollux, Spica Virginis, Antares, Fomalhaut, Arided (Alpha Cygni), and Regulus, the well-known double star Castor following not far behind Regulus. The second magnitude embraces, according to Argelander, 65 stars; the third, 190; fourth, 425; fifth, 1,100; sixth, 3,200; while for the ninth magnitude the number leaps up to 142,000. It is thus seen that the number of stars increases with enormous rapidity as the smaller magnitudes come into question, and, according to Newcomb, there is no evidence of any falling off in the ratio of increase up to the tenth magnitude. In the smaller magnitudes, however, the ratio of increase does not maintain itself. The number of the stars, though very great, is not infinite.

A further fact which quickly becomes apparent to the naked eye is that the stars are not all of the same colour. Sirius, for example, is of a brilliant white, with a steely glitter; Betelgeux, comparatively near to it in the sky, is of a beautiful topaz tint, perhaps on the whole the most exquisite single star in the sky, so far as regards colour; Aldebaran is orange-yellow, while Vega is white with a bluish cast, as is also Rigel. These diversities become much more apparent when the telescope is employed. At the same time the observer may be warned against expecting too much in the way of colour, for, as a matter of fact, the colours of the stars, while perfectly manifest, are yet of great delicacy, and it is difficult to describe them in ordinary terms without some suspicion of exaggeration. Stars of a reddish tone, which ranges from the merest shade of orange-yellow up to a fairly deep orange, are not uncommon; several first-magnitude stars, as already noted, have distinct orange tones. For anything approaching to real blues and greens, we must go to the smaller stars, and the finest examples of blue or green stars are found in the smaller members of some of the double systems. Thus in the case of the double Beta Cygni (Albireo), one of the most beautiful and easy telescopic objects in the northern sky, the larger star is orange-yellow, and the smaller blue; in that of Gamma Andromedæ the larger is yellow, and the smaller bluish-green; while Gamma Leonis has a large yellow star, and a small greenish-yellow one in connection. The student who desires to pursue the subject of star colours should possess himself of the catalogue published in the Memoirs of the British Astronomical Association, which gives the colours of the lucid stars determined from the mean of a very large number of observations made by different observers.

In this connection it may be noticed that there is some suspicion that the colours of certain stars have changed within historic times, or at least that they have not the same colour now which they are said to have had in former days. The evidence is not in any instance strong enough to warrant the assertion that actual change has taken place; but it is perfectly natural to suppose that it does, and indeed must gradually progress. As the stars are intensely hot bodies, there must have been periods when their heat was gradually rising to its maximum, and there must be periods when they will gradually cool off to extinction, and these stages must be represented by changes in the colour of the particular star in question. In all probability, then, the colour of a star gives some indication of the stage to which it has advanced in its life-history; and as a matter of fact, this proves to be so, the colour of a star being found to be generally a fair indication of what its constitution, as revealed by the spectroscope, will be.

Another feature of the stars which cannot fail to be noticed is the fact that they are not evenly distributed over the heavens, but are grouped into a variety of configurations or constellations. In the very dawn of human history these configurations woke the imaginations of the earliest star-gazers, and fanciful shapes and titles were attached to the star-groups, which have been handed down to the present time, and are still in use. It must be confessed that in some cases it takes a very lively imagination to find any resemblance between the constellation and the figure which has been associated with it. The anatomy of Pegasus, for example, would scarcely commend itself to a horse-breeder, while the student will look in vain for any resemblance to a human figure, heroic or unheroic, in the straggling group of stars which bears the name of Hercules. At the same time a few of the constellations do more or less resemble the objects from which their titles are derived. Thus the figure of a man may without any great difficulty be traced among the brilliant stars which form the beautiful constellation Orion; while Delphinus presents at least an approximation to a fish-like form, and Corona Borealis gives the half of a diadem of sparkling jewels.

A knowledge of the constellations, and, if possible, of the curious old myths and legends attaching to them, should form part of the equipment of every educated person; yet very few people can tell one group from another, much less say what constellations are visible at a given hour at any particular season of the year. People who are content merely to gape at the heavens in 'a wonderful clear night of stars' little know how much interest they are losing. When the constellations and the chief stars are learned and kept in memory, the face of the sky becomes instinct with interest, and each successive season brings with it the return of some familiar group which is hailed as one hails an old friend. Nor is the task of becoming familiar with the constellations one of any difficulty. Indeed, there are few pleasanter tasks than to trace out the figures of the old heroes and heroines of mythology by the help of a simple star-map, and once learned, they need never be forgotten. In this branch of the subject there are many easily accessible helps. For a simple guide, Peck's 'Constellations and how to Find Them' is both cheap and useful, while Newcomb's 'Astronomy for Everybody' and Maunder's 'Astronomy without a Telescope' also give careful and simple directions. Maunder's volume is particularly useful for a beginner, combining, as it does, most careful instructions as to the tracing of the constellations with a set of clear and simple star-charts, and a most interesting discussion of the origin of these ancient star-groups. A list of the northern constellations with a few of the most notable objects of interest in each will be found in Appendix II.

Winding among the constellations, and forming a gigantic belt round the whole star-sphere, lies that most wonderful feature of the heavens familiar to all under the name of the Milky Way. This great luminous girdle of the sky may be seen in some portion of its extent, and at some hour of the night, at all seasons of the year, though in May it is somewhat inconveniently placed for observation. Roughly speaking, it presents the appearance of a broad arch or pathway of misty light, 'whose groundwork is of stars'; but the slightest attention will reveal the fact that in reality its structure is of great complexity. It throws out streamers on either side and at all angles, condenses at various points into cloudy masses of much greater brilliancy than the average, strangely pierced sometimes by dark gaps through which we seem to look into infinite and almost tenantless space (Plate XXVII.), while in other quarters it spreads away in considerable width, and to such a degree of faintness that the eye can scarcely tell where it ends. At a point in the constellation Cygnus, well seen during autumn and the early months of winter, it splits up into two great branches which run separate to the Southern horizon with a well-marked dark gap dividing them.

When examined with any telescopic power, the Milky Way reveals itself as a wonderful collection of stars and star-clusters; and it will also be found that there is a very remarkable tendency among the stars to gather in the neighbourhood of this great starry belt. So much is this case that, in the words of Professor Newcomb, 'Were the cloud-forms which make up the Milky Way invisible to us, we should still be able to mark out its course by the crowding of the lucid stars towards it.' Not less remarkable is the fact that the distribution of the nebulæ with regard to the Galaxy is precisely the opposite of that of the stars. There are, of course, many nebulæ in the Galaxy; but, at the same time, they are comparatively less numerous along its course, and grow more and more numerous in proportion as we depart from it. It seems impossible to avoid the conclusion that these twin facts are intimately related to one another, though the explanation of them is not yet forthcoming.

In the year 1665 the famous astronomer Hooke wrote concerning the small star Gamma Arietis: 'I took notice that it consisted of two small stars very near together; a like instance of which I have not else met with in all the heavens.' This is the first English record of the observation of a double star, though Riccioli detected the duplicity of Zeta Ursæ Majoris (Mizar), in 1650, and Huygens saw three stars in Theta Orionis in 1656. These were the earliest beginnings of double-star observation, which has since grown to such proportions that double stars are now numbered in the heavens by thousands. Of course, certain stars appear to be double even when viewed with the unaided eye. Thus Mizar, a bright star in the handle of the Plough, referred to above, has not far from it a fainter companion known as Alcor, which the Arabs used to consider a test of vision. Either it has brightened in modern times, or else the Arabs have received too much credit for keenness of sight, for Mizar and Alcor now make a pair that is quite easy to very ordinary sight even in our turbid atmosphere. Alpha Capricorni, and Zeta Ceti, with Iota Orionis are also instances of naked-eye doubles, while exceptionally keen sight will detect that the star Epsilon Lyræ, which forms a little triangle with the brilliant Vega and Zeta Lyræ, is double, or at least that it is not single, but slightly elongated in form. Astronomers, however, would not call such objects as these 'double stars' at all; they reserve that title for stars which are very much closer together than the components of a naked-eye double can ever be. The last-mentioned star, Epsilon Lyræ, affords a very good example of the distinction. To the naked eye it is, generally speaking, not to be distinguished from a single star. Keen sight elongates it; exceptionally keen sight divides it into two stars extremely close to one another. But on using even a very moderate telescope, say a 2½-inch with a power of 100 or upwards, the two stars which the keenest sight could barely separate are seen widely apart in the field, while each of them has in its turn split up into two little dots of light. Thus, to the telescope, Epsilon Lyræ is really a quadruple star, while in addition there is a faint star forming a triangle with the two pairs, and a large instrument will reveal two very faint stars, the 'debilissima,' one on either side of the line joining the larger stars. These I have seen with 3⅞-inch.

What the telescope does with Epsilon Lyræ, it does with a great multitude of other stars. There are thousands of doubles of all degrees of easiness and difficulty—doubles wide apart, and doubles so close that only the finest telescopes in the world can separate them; doubles of every degree of likeness or of disparity in their components, from Alpha Geminorum (Castor), with its two beautiful stars of almost equal lustre, to Sirius, where the chief star is the brightest in all the heavens, and the companion so small, or rather so faint, that it takes a very fine glass to pick it out in the glare of its great primary. The student will find in these double stars an extremely good series of tests for the quality of his telescope. They are, further, generally objects of great beauty, being often characterized, as already mentioned, by diversity of colour in the two components. Thus, in addition to the examples given above, Eta Cassiopeiæ presents the beautiful picture of a yellow star in conjunction with a red one, while Epsilon Boötis has been described as 'most beautiful yellow and superb blue,' and Alpha Herculis consists of an orange star close to one which is emerald green. It has been suggested that the colours in such instances are merely complementary, the impression of orange or yellow in the one star producing a purely subjective impression of blue or green when the other is viewed; but it has been conclusively proved that the colours of very many of the smaller stars in such cases are actual and inherent.

Not only are there thousands of double stars in the heavens, but there are also many multiple stars, where the telescope splits an apparently single star up into three, four, or sometimes six or seven separate stars. Of these multiples, one of the best known is Theta Orionis. It is the middle star of the sword which hangs from the belt of Orion, and is, of course, notable from its connection with the Great Nebula; but it is also a very beautiful multiple star. A 2½-inch telescope will show that it consists of four stars in the form of a trapezium; large instruments show two excessively faint stars in addition. Again, in the same constellation lies Sigma Orionis, immediately below the lowermost star of the giant's belt. In a 3-inch telescope this star splits up into a beautiful multiple of six components, their differences in size and tint making the little group a charming object.

Looking at the multitude of double and multiple stars, the question can scarcely fail to suggest itself: Is there any real connection between the stars which thus appear so close to one another? It can be readily understood that the mere fact of their appearing close together in the field of the telescope does not necessarily imply real closeness. Two gas-lamps, for instance, may appear quite close together to an observer who is at some distance from them, when in reality they may be widely separated one from the other—the apparent closeness being due to the fact that they are almost in the same line of sight. No doubt many of the stars which appear double in the telescope are of this class—'optical doubles,' as they are called, and are in reality separated by vast distances from one another. But the great majority have not only an apparent, but also a real closeness; and in a number of cases this is proved by the fact that observation shows the stars in question to be physically connected, and to revolve around a common centre of gravity. Double stars which are thus physically connected are known as 'binaries.' The discovery of the existence of this real connection between some double stars is due, like so many of the most interesting astronomical discoveries, to Sir William Herschel. At present the number of stars known to be binary is somewhat under one thousand; but in the case of most of these, the revolution round a common centre which proves their physical connection is extremely slow, and consequently the majority of binary stars have as yet been followed only through a small portion of their orbits, and the change of position sufficient to enable a satisfactory orbit to be computed has occurred in only a small proportion of the total number. The first binary star to have its orbit computed was Xi Ursæ Majoris, whose revolution of about sixty years has been twice completed since, in 1780, Sir William Herschel discovered it to be double.

The star which has the shortest period at present known is the fourth magnitude Delta Equulei, which has a fifth magnitude companion. The pair complete their revolution, according to Hussey, in 5·7 years. Kappa Pegasi comes next in speed of revolution, with a period of eleven and a half years, while the star 85 of the same constellation takes rather more than twice as long to complete its orbit. From such swiftly circling pairs as these, the periods range up to hundreds of years. Thus, for example, the well-known double star Castor, probably the most beautiful double in the northern heavens, and certainly the best object of its class for a small telescope, is held to have a period of 347 years, which, though long enough, is a considerable reduction upon the 1,000 once attributed to it.

But the number of binary stars known is not confined to those which have been discovered and measured by means of the telescope and micrometer. One of the most wonderful results of modern astronomical research has been the discovery of the fact that many stars have revolving round them invisible companions, which are either dark bodies, or else are so close to their primaries as for ever to defy the separating powers of our telescopes. The discovery of these dark, or at least invisible, companions is one of the most remarkable triumphs of the spectroscope. It was in 1888 that Vogel first applied the spectroscopic method to the well-known variable star, Beta Persei —known as Algol, 'the Demon,' from its 'slowly-winking eye.' The variation in the light of Algol is very large, from second to fourth magnitude; Vogel therefore reasoned that if this variation were caused by a dark companion partially eclipsing the bright star, the companion must be sufficiently large to cause motion in Algol—that is, to cause both stars to revolve round a common centre of gravity. Should this be the case, then at one point of its orbit Algol must be approaching, and at the opposite point receding from the earth; and therefore the shift of the lines of its spectrum towards the violet in the one instance and towards the red in the other would settle the question of whether it had or had not an invisible companion. The spectroscopic evidence proved quite conclusive. It was found that before its eclipses, Algol was receding from the sun at the rate of $26\frac{1}{3}$ miles per second, while after eclipse there was a similar motion of approach; and therefore the hypothesis of an invisible companion was proved to be fact. Vogel carried his researches further, his inquiry into the questions of the size and distance apart of the two bodies leading him to the conclusion that the bright star is rather more, and its companion rather less than 1,000,000 miles in diameter; while the distance which divides them is somewhat more than 3,000,000 miles. Though larger, both bodies prove to be less massive than our sun, Algol being estimated at four-ninths and its companion at two-ninths of the solar mass.

The class of double star disclosed in this manner is known as the 'spectroscopic binary,' and has various other types differing from the Algol type. Thus the type of which Xi Ursæ Majoris was the first detected instance has two component bodies not differing greatly in brightness from one another. In such a case the fact of the star being binary is revealed through the consideration that in any binary system the two components must necessarily always be moving in opposite directions. Hence the shift of the lines of their spectrum will be in opposite directions also, and when one of the stars (A) is moving towards us, and the other (B) away from us, all the lines of the spectrum which are common to the two will appear double, those of A being displaced towards the violet and those of B towards the red. After a quarter of a revolution, when the stars are momentarily in a straight line with us, the lines will all appear single; but after half a revolution they will again be displaced, those of A this time towards the red and those of B towards the violet.

There has thus been opened up an entirely new field of research, and the idea, long cherished, that the stars might prove to have dark, or, at all events, invisible, companions attendant on them, somewhat as our own sun has its planets, has been proved to be perfectly sound. So far, in the case of dark companions, only bodies of such vast size have been detected as to render any comparison with the planets of our system difficult; but the principle is established, and the probability of great numbers of the stars having real planetary systems attendant on them is so great as to become practically a certainty. 'We naturally infer,' says Professor Newcomb, 'that ... innumerable stars may have satellites, planets, or companion stars so close or so faint as to elude our powers of observation.'

From the consideration of spectroscopic binaries we naturally turn to that of variable stars, the two classes being, to some extent at least, coincident, as is evidenced by the case of Algol. While the discovery of spectroscopic binaries is one of the latest results of research, that of variability among stars dates from comparatively far back in the history of astronomy. As early as the year 1596 David Fabricius noted the star now known as Omicron Ceti, or Mira, 'the Wonderful,' as being of the third magnitude, while in the following year he found that it had vanished. A succession of appearances and disappearances was witnessed in the middle of the next century by Holwarda, and from that time the star has been kept under careful observation, and its variations have been determined with some exactness, though there are anomalies as yet unexplained. 'Once in eleven months,' writes Miss Clerke, 'the star mounts up in about 125 days from below the ninth to near the third, or even to the second magnitude; then, after a pause of two or three weeks, drops again to its former low level in once and a half times, on an average, the duration of its rise.' This most extraordinary fluctuation means that at a bright maximum Mira emits 1,500 times as much light as at a low minimum. The star thus subject to such remarkable outbursts is, like most variables, of a reddish colour, and at maximum its spectrum shows the presence of glowing hydrogen. Its average period is about 331 days; but this period is subject to various irregularities, and the maximum has sometimes been as much as two months away from the predicted time. Mira Ceti may be taken as the type of the numerous class of stars known as 'long-period variables.'

Not less interesting are those stars whose variations cover only short periods, extending from less than thirty days down to a few hours. Of these, perhaps the most easily observed, as it is also one of the most remarkable, is Beta Lyræ. This star is one of the two bright stars of nearly equal magnitude which form an obtuse-angled triangle with the brilliant first-magnitude star Vega. The other star of the pair is Gamma Lyræ, and between them lies the famous Ring Nebula, to be referred to later. Ordinarily Beta Lyræ is of magnitude 3·4, but from this it passes, in a period of rather less than thirteen days, through two minima, in one of which it descends to magnitude 3·9 and in the other to 4·5. This fluctuation seems trifling. It really means, however, that at maximum the star is two and three-quarter times brighter than when it sinks to magnitude 4·5; and the variation can be easily recognised by the naked eye, owing to the fact of the nearness of so convenient a comparison star as Gamma Lyræ. Beta Lyræ is a member of the class of spectroscopic binaries, and belongs to that type of the class in which the mutually eclipsing bodies are both bright. In such cases the variation in brilliancy is caused by the fact that when the two bodies are, so to speak, side by side, light is received from both of them, and a maximum is observed; while, when they are end on, both in line with ourselves, one cuts off more or less of the other's light from us, thus causing a minimum.

A third class, distinct from either of the preceding, is that of the Algol Variables, so-called from the bright star Beta Persei, which has already been mentioned as a spectroscopic binary. Than this star there is no more notable variable in the heavens, and its situation fortunately renders it peculiarly easy of observation to northern students. Algol shines for about fifty-nine hours as a star of small second magnitude, then suddenly begins to lose light, and in four and a half hours has fallen to magnitude three and a half, losing in so short a space two-thirds of its normal brilliancy. It remains in this degraded condition for only fifteen minutes, and then begins to recover, reaching its normal lustre in about five hours more. These remarkable changes, due, as before mentioned, to the presence of an invisible eclipsing companion, are gone through with the utmost regularity, so much so that, as Gore says, the minima of Algol 'can be predicted with as much certainty as an eclipse of the sun.' The features of the type-star are more or less closely reproduced in the other Algol Variables—a comparatively long period of steady light emission, followed by a rapid fall to one or more minima, and a rapid recovery of light. The class as yet is a small one, but new members are gradually being added to it, the majority of them white, like the type-star.

The study of variable stars is one which should seem to be specially reserved for the amateur observer. In general, it requires but little instrumental equipment. Many variables can be seen at maximum, some even at minimum, with the unaided eye; in other cases a good opera or field glass is all that is required, and a 2½ or 3-inch telescope will enable the observer to command quite an extensive field of work. Here, again, the beginner may be referred to the *Memoirs* of the British Astronomical Association for help and guidance, and may be advised to connect himself with the Variable Star Section.

With the exception of such variations in the lustre of certain stars as have been described, the aspect of the heavens is, in general, fixed and unchanging. There are, as we shall see, real changes of the vastest importance continually going on; but the distances separating us from the fixed stars are so enormous that these changes shrink into nothingness, and the astronomers of forty centuries before our era would find comparatively little change today in the aspect of the constellations with which they were familiar. But occasionally a very remarkable change does take place, in the apparition of a new or temporary star. The accounts of the appearance of such objects are not very numerous, but are of great interest. We pass over those recorded, in more or less casual fashion, by the ancients, for the reason that the descriptions given are in general more picturesque than illuminative. It does not add much to one's knowledge, though it may excite wonder, to find the Chinese annals recording the appearance, in A.D. 173, of a new star 'resembling a large bamboo mat!'

The first Nova, of which we have a really scientific record, was the star which suddenly blazed out, in November, 1572, in the familiar W of Cassiopeia. It was carefully observed by the great astronomer, Tycho Brahé, and, according to him, was brighter than Sirius, Alpha Lyræ, or Jupiter. Tycho followed it till March, 1574, by which time it had sunk to the limit of unaided vision, and further observation became impossible. There is at present a star of the eleventh magnitude close to the place fixed for the Nova from Tycho's observations. In 1604 and 1670, new stars were observed, the first by Kepler and his assistants, the second by the monk Anthelme; but from 1670 there was a long break in the list of discoveries, which was ended by Hind's observation of a new star in Ophiuchus (April, 1848). This was never a very conspicuous object, rising only to somewhat less than fourth magnitude, and soon fading to tenth or eleventh. We can only mention the 'Blaze Star' of Corona Borealis, discovered by Birmingham in 1866, the Nova discovered in 1876 by Schmidt of Athens, near Rho Cygni—an object which seems to have faded out into a planetary nebula, a fate apparently characteristic of this class of star—and the star which appeared in 1885, close to the nucleus of the Great Nebula in Andromeda.

In 1892, Dr. Anderson of Edinburgh discovered in the constellation Auriga a star which he estimated as of fifth magnitude. The discovery was made on January 31, and the new star was found to have been photographed at Harvard on plates taken from December 16, 1891, to January 31, 1892. Apparently this Nova differed from other temporary stars in the fact that it attained its full brightness only gradually. By February 3 it rose to magnitude 3·5, then faded by April 1 to fifteenth, but in August brightened up again to about ninth magnitude. It is now visible as a small star. The great development of spectroscopic resources brought this object, otherwise not a very conspicuous one, under the closest scrutiny. Its spectrum showed many bright lines, which were accompanied by dark ones on the side next the blue. The idea was thus suggested that the outburst of brilliancy was due to a collision between two bodies, one of which, that causing the dark lines, was approaching the earth, while the other was receding from it. Lockyer considered the conflagration to be due to a collision between two swarms of meteorites, Huggins that it was caused by the near approach to one another of two gaseous bodies, while others suggested that the rush of a star or of a swarm of meteorites through a nebula would explain the facts observed. Subsequent observations of the spectrum of Nova Aurigæ have revealed the fact that it has obeyed the destiny which seems to wait on temporary stars, having become a planetary nebula.

Dr. Anderson followed up his first achievement by the discovery of a brilliant Nova in the constellation Perseus. The discovery was made on the night of February 21-22, 1901, the star being then of magnitude 2·7. Within two days it became about the third brightest star in the sky, being a little more brilliant than Capella; but before the middle of April it had sunk to fifth magnitude. The rapidity of its rise must have been phenomenal! A plate exposed at Harvard on February 19, and showing stars to the eleventh magnitude, bore no trace of the Nova. 'It must therefore,' says Newcomb, 'have risen from some magnitude below the eleventh to the first within about three days. This difference corresponds to an increase of the light ten thousandfold!' Such a statement leaves the mind simply appalled before the spectacle of a cataclysm so infinitely transcending the very wildest dreams of fancy. Subsequent observations have shown the usual tendency towards development into a nebula, and in August, 1901, photographs were actually obtained of a nebulosity round the star, showing remarkable condensations. These photographs, taken at Yerkes Observatory, when compared with others taken at Mount Hamilton in November, revealed the startling fact that the condensations of the nebula were apparently in extraordinarily rapid motion. Now the Nova shows no appreciable parallax, or in other words is so distant that its distance cannot be measured; on what scale, therefore, must these motions have been to be recorded plainly across a gulf measurable perhaps in hundreds of light years!

Nova Geminorum, discovered by Professor Turner, at Oxford, in March, 1903, had not the striking features which lent so much interest to Nova Persei. It showed a crimson colour, and its spectrum indicated the presence in its blaze of hydrogen and helium; but it faded so rapidly as to show that the disturbance affected a comparatively small body, and it has exhibited the familiar new star change into a nebula.

One point with regard to the Novæ in Auriga and Perseus deserves notice. These discoveries, so remarkable in themselves, and so fruitful in the extension of our knowledge, were made by an amateur observer with no greater equipment than a small pocket telescope and a Klein's Star-Atlas. The thorough knowledge of the face of the heavens which enabled Dr. Anderson to pick out the faint glimmer of Nova Aurigæ and to be certain that the star was a new one is not in the least unattainable by anyone who cares to give time and patience to its acquisition; and even should the study never be rewarded by a capture so dramatic as that of Nova Persei, the familiarity gained in its course with the beauty and wonder of the star-sphere will in itself be an ample reward.

# CHAPTER XV

## CLUSTERS AND NEBULÆ

Even the most casual observer of the heavens cannot have failed to notice that in certain instances the stars are grouped so closely together as to form well-marked clusters. The most familiar example is the well-known group of the Pleiades, in the constellation Taurus, while quite close is the more scattered group of the Hyades. Another somewhat coarsely scattered group is that known as Coma Berenices, the Hair of Berenice, which lies beneath the handle of the Plough; and a fainter group is the cluster Præsepe, which lies in the inconspicuous constellation Cancer, between Gemini and Leo, appearing to the naked eye like a fairly bright, hazy patch, which the smallest telescope resolves into a cloud of faint stars.

**PLATE XXVIII.**

1.

## 2.

Irregular Star Clusters. Photographed by E. E. Barnard.

1. Messier 35 in Gemini.     2. Double Cluster in Perseus.

The Pleiades form undoubtedly the most remarkable naked-eye group in the heavens. The six stars which are visible to average eyesight are Alcyone, 3rd magnitude; Maia, Electra, and Atlas, of the 4th; Merope, 4⅓; and Taygeta, 4½. While Celæno, 5⅓; Pleione, 5½; and Asterope, 6, hang on the verge of visibility. With an opera-glass about thirty more may be counted, while photographs show between 2,000 and 3,000. It is probable that the fainter stars have no real connection with the cluster itself, which is merely seen upon a background of more distant star-dust. Modern photographs have shown that this cluster is involved in a great nebula, which stretches in curious wisps and straight lines from star to star, and surrounds the whole group. The Pleiades make a brilliant object for a small telescope with a low magnifying power, but are too scattered for an instrument of any size to be effective upon them. The finest of all irregular star-clusters is that known as the Sword-handle of Perseus. Midway between Perseus and the W of Cassiopeia, and directly in the line of the Galaxy, the eye discerns a small, hazy patch of light, of which even a 2 or 3 inch glass will make a beautiful object, while with a large aperture its splendour is extraordinary. It consists of two groups of stars which are both in the same field with a small instrument and low powers. Towards the edge of the field the stars are comparatively sparsely scattered; but towards the two centres of condensation the thickness of grouping steadily increases. Altogether there is no more impressive stellar object than this magnificent double cluster (Plate XXVIII., 2). Another very fine example of the irregular type of grouping is seen in M. 35, situated in the constellation Gemini, and forming an obtuse-angled triangle with the stars Mu and Eta Geminorum (Plate XXVIII., 1). There are many other similar groups fairly well within the reach of comparatively small instruments, and some of these are mentioned in the list of objects (Appendix II.).

Still more remarkable than the irregular clusters are those which condense into a more or less globular form. There are not very many objects of this class in the northern sky visible with a small telescope, but the beauty of those which are visible is very notable. The most splendid of all is the famous cluster M. 13 Herculis. (The M. in these cases refers to the catalogue of such objects drawn up by Messier, the French 'comet ferret,' to guide him in his labours.) M. 13 is situated almost on the line between Zeta and Eta Herculis, and at about two-thirds of the distance from Zeta towards Eta. It is faintly visible to the unaided eye when its place is known, and, when viewed with sufficient telescopic power, is a very fine object. Nichol's remark that 'perhaps no one ever saw it for the first time through a large telescope without uttering a shout of wonder' seems to be based on a somewhat extravagant estimate of the enthusiasm and demonstrativeness of the average star-gazer; but the cluster is a very noble object all the same, consisting, according to a count made on a negative taken in 1899, of no fewer than 5,482 stars, which condense towards the centre into a mass of great brilliancy. It takes a large aperture to resolve the centre of the cluster into stars, but even a 3-inch will show a number of twinkling points of light in the outlying streamers (Plate XXIX.). In the same constellation will also be found the cluster M. 92, similar to, but somewhat fainter than M. 13; and other globular clusters are noted in the Appendix. Most of these objects, however, can only be seen after a fashion with small instruments. Of the true nature and condition of these wonderful aggregations we are so far profoundly ignorant. The question of whether they are composed of small stars, situated at no very great distance from the earth, or of large bodies, which are rendered faint to our vision by immense distance, has been frequently discussed. Gore concludes that they are 'composed of stars of average size and mass, and that the faintness of the component stars is simply due to their immense distance from the earth.' If so, the true proportions of some of these clusters must be indeed phenomenal! A very remarkable feature to be noticed in connection with some of them is the high proportion of variable stars which they contain. Professor Bailey has found that in such clusters as M. 3 and M. 5 the proportion of variables is one in seven and one in eleven respectively, while several other groups show proportions ranging from one in eighteen up to one in sixty. As the general proportion of variables is somewhere about one in a hundred, these ratios are remarkable. They only characterize a certain number of clusters, however, and are absent in cases which seem strictly parallel to others where they exist.

**PLATE XXIX.**

Cluster M. 13 Herculis. Photographed by Mr. W. E. Wilson.

We now pass from the star-clusters to the nebulæ properly so called. Till after the middle of last century it was an open question whether there was any real distinction between the two classes of bodies. Herschel had suggested the existence of a 'shining fluid,' distributed through space, whose condensations gave rise to those objects known as nebulæ; but it was freely maintained by many that the objects which could not be resolved into stars were irresolvable only because of their vast distance, and that the increase of telescopic power would result in the disclosure of their stellar nature. This view seemed to be confirmed when it was confidently announced that the great Rosse telescope had effected the resolution of the Orion Nebula, which was looked upon as being in some sort a test case. But the supposed proof of the stellar character of nebulæ did not hold its ground for long, for in 1864 Sir William Huggins, on applying the spectroscope to the planetary nebula in Draco, found that its spectrum consisted merely of bright lines, one of which—the most conspicuous—was close to the position of a nitrogen line, but has proved to be distinct from it; while of the other two, one was unmistakably the F line of hydrogen and the other remains still unidentified. Thus it became immediately manifest that the nebula in Draco did not consist of distant stars, but was of gaseous constitution; and Sir William Herschel's idea of the existence of non-stellar matter in the universe was abundantly justified. Subsequent research has proved that multitudes of nebulæ yield a bright-line spectrum, and are therefore gaseous. Of these, by far the most remarkable and interesting is the Great Nebula of Orion. The observer will readily distinguish even with the unaided eye that the middle star of the three that form the sword which hangs down from Orion's belt has a somewhat hazy appearance. A small telescope reveals the fact that the haziness is due to the presence of a great misty cloud of light, in shape something like a fish-mouth, and of a greenish colour. At the junction of the jaws lies the multiple star Theta Orionis, which with a 2- or 3-inch glass appears to consist of four stars—'the trapezium'—large instruments showing in addition two very faint stars.

With greater telescopic power additional features begin to reveal themselves; the mist immediately above the trapezium assumes a roughly triangular shape, and is evidently much denser than the rest of the nebula, presenting a curdled appearance similar to that of the stretches of small cloud in a 'mackerel' sky; while from the upper jaw of the fish-mouth a great shadowy horn rises and stretches upward, until it gradually loses itself in the darkness of the background. This wonderful nebula appears to have been discovered in 1618, but was first really described and sketched by Huygens in 1656, since when it has been kept under the closest scrutiny, innumerable drawings of it having been made and compared from time to time with the view of detecting any traces of change. The finest drawings extant are those of Sir John Herschel and Mr. Lassell, and the elaborate one made with the help of the Rosse 6-foot mirror.

Drawing, however, at no time a satisfactory method of representing the shadowy and elusive forms of nebulæ, has now been entirely superseded by the work of the sensitive plate. Common, Roberts, Pickering, and others have succeeded admirably in photographing the Great Nebula with exposures ranging from half an hour up to six hours. The extension of nebulous matter revealed by these photographs is enormous (Plate XXX.), so much so that many of the central features of the nebula with which the eye is familiar are quite masked and overpowered in the photographic print. The spectrum of the Orion Nebula exhibits indications of the presence of hydrogen and helium, as well as the characteristic green ray which marks the unknown substance named 'nebulium.'

The appearance of this 'tumultuous cloud, instinct with fire and nitre,' is always amazing. Sir Robert Ball considers it one of the three most remarkable objects visible in the northern heavens, the other two being Saturn and the Great Cluster in Hercules. But, beautiful and wonderful as both of these may be, the Orion Nebula conveys to the mind a sense of mystery which the others, in spite of their extraordinary features, never suggest. Absolutely staggering is the thought of the stupendous dimensions of the nebula. Professor Pickering considers its parallax to be so small as to indicate a distance of not less than 1,000 years light journey from our earth! It is almost impossible to realize the meaning of such a statement. When we look at this shining mist, we are seeing it, not as it is now, but as it was more than a hundred years before the Norman Conquest; were it blotted out of existence now, it would still shine to us and our descendants for another ten centuries in virtue of the rays of light which are already speeding across the vast gulf that separates our world from its curdled clouds of fire-mist, and the astronomers of A.D. 2906 might still be speculating on the nature and destiny of a thing which for ages had been non-existent! That an object should be visible at all at such a distance demands dimensions which are really incomprehensible; but the Orion Nebula is not only visible, it is conspicuous!

**PLATE XXX.**

Photograph of the Orion Nebula (W. H. Pickering).

The rival of this famous nebula in point of visibility is the well-known spiral in the girdle of Andromeda. On a clear night it can easily be seen with the naked eye near the star Nu Andromedæ, and may readily be, as it has often been, mistaken for a comet. Its discovery must, therefore, have been practically coincident with the beginnings of human observation of the heavens; but special mention of it does not occur before the tenth century of our era. A small telescope will show it fairly well, but it must be admitted that the first view is apt to produce a feeling of disappointment. The observer need not look for anything like the whirling streams of light which are revealed on modern long exposure photographs (Plate XXXI., 1). He will see what Simon Marius so aptly described under the simile of 'the light seen from a great distance through half-transparent horn plates'—a lens-shaped misty light, brightening very rapidly towards a nucleus which seems always on the point of coming to definition but is never defined, and again fading away without traceable boundary into obscurity on every side. The first step towards an explanation of the structure of this curious object was made by Bond in the middle of last century. With the 15-inch refractor of the Cambridge (U.S.A.) Observatory, he detected two dark rifts running lengthwise through the bright matter of the nebula; but it was not till 1887 and 1888 that its true form was revealed by Roberts's photographs. It was then seen to be a gigantic spiral or whirlpool, the rifts noticed by Bond being the lines of separation between the huge whorls of the spiral. Of course, small instruments are powerless to reveal anything of this wonderful structure; still there is an interest in being able to see, however imperfectly, an object which seems to present to our eyes the embodiment of that process by which some assume that our own system may have been shaped. So far as the powers of the best telescopes go, the Andromeda Nebula presents no appearance of stellar constitution. Its spectrum, according to Scheiner, is continuous, which would imply that in spite of appearances it is in reality composed of stars; but Sir William Huggins has seen also bright lines in it. Possibly it may represent a stage intermediate between the stellar and the gaseous.

**PLATE XXXI.**

North.

1.

North.

2.

Photographs of Spiral Nebulæ. By Dr. Max Wolf.

1. Great Nebula in Andromeda.     2. Spiral in Triangulum (M. 33).

Another remarkable example of a spiral nebula will be found in M. 51. It is situated in the constellation Canes Venatici, and may be easily picked up, being not far from the end star of the Plough-handle Eta Ursæ Majoris. This strange object, 'gyre on gyre' of fire-mist, was one of the first spirals to have its true character demonstrated by the Rosse telescope. It is visible with moderate optical powers, but displays to them none of that marvellous structure which the great 6-foot mirror revealed for the first time, and which has been amply confirmed by subsequent photographic evidence (Plate XXXII.).

**PLATE XXXII.**

Photograph of Whirlpool Nebula (M. 51). Taken by Mr. W. E. Wilson, March 6, 1897.

Among other classes of nebulæ we can only mention the ring and the planetary. Of each of these, one good example can be seen, though, it must be admitted, not much more than seen, with very modest instrumental equipment. Midway between the two stars Beta and Gamma Lyræ, already referred to in connection with the variability of the former, the observer by a little fishing will find the famous Ring Nebula of Lyra. With low powers it appears simply as a hazy oval spot; but it bears magnifying moderately well, and its annular shape comes out fairly with a power of eighty on a 2½ inch, though it can scarcely be called a brilliant object with that aperture, or indeed with anything much under 8 inches. None the less, it is of great interest, the curious symmetry of this gaseous ring making it an almost unique object. It resembles nothing so much as those vortex rings which an expert smoker will sometimes send quivering through the air. Photographs show clearly a star within the ring, and this star has a very curious history, having been frequently visible in comparatively small telescopes, and again, within a year or two, invisible in much larger ones. Photography seems to have succeeded in persuading it to forgo these caprices, though it presents peculiarities of light which are still unexplained. The actinic plate reveals also very clearly that deficiency of light at the ends of the longer diameter of the ring which

171

can be detected, though with more difficulty, by the eye. The class of annular nebulæ is not a large one, and none of its other members come within the effective range of small instruments.

Planetary nebulæ are so called because with ordinary powers they present somewhat of the appearance of a planet seen very dimly and considerably out of focus. The appearance of uniformity in their boundaries vanishes under higher telescopic power, and they appear to be generally decidedly elliptical; they yield a gaseous spectrum with strong evidence of the presence of 'nebulium,' the unknown substance which gives evidence of its presence in the spectrum of every true nebula, and has, so far (with one doubtful exception) been found nowhere else. The chief example of the class is that body in Draco which first yielded to Huggins the secret of the gaseous nature of the nebulæ. It lies nearly half-way between Polaris and Gamma Draconis, and is described by Webb as a 'very luminous disc, much like a considerable star out of focus.' It is by no means a striking object, but has its own interest as the first witness to the true nature of that great class of heavenly bodies to which it belongs.

The multitude of nebulous bodies scattered over the heavens may be judged from the fact that Professor Keeler, after partial surveys carried out by means of photography with the Crossley reflector, came to the conclusion that the number within the reach of that instrument (36-inch aperture) might be put down at not less than 120,000. It is a curious fact that the grouping of this great multitude seems to be fundamentally different from that of the stars. Where stars are densely scattered, nebulæ are comparatively scarce; where nebulæ abound, the stars are less thickly sown. So much is this the case, that, when Herschel in his historic 'sweeps' of the heavens came across a notably starless region, he used to call out to his assistant to 'prepare for nebulæ.' The idea of a physical connection between the two classes of bodies is thus underlined in a manner which, as Herbert Spencer saw so early as 1854, is quite unmistakable.

There remain one or two questions of which the very shortest notice must suffice—not because they are unimportant, but because their importance is such that any attempt at adequate discussion of them is impossible in our limited space. One of these inevitably rises to the mind in presence of the myriads of the heavenly host—the familiar question which was so pleasingly suggested to our growing minds by the nursery rhyme of our childhood. To the question, What is a star? it has now become possible to give an answer which is satisfactory so far as it goes, though it is in a very rudimentary stage as regards details.

The spectroscope has taught us that the stars consist of incandescent solid bodies, or of masses of incandescent gas so large and dense as not to be transparent; and further, that they are surrounded by atmospheres consisting of gases cooler than themselves. The nature of the substances incandescent in the individual bodies has also to some extent been learned. The result has been to show that, while there is considerable variety in the chemical constitution and condition of the stars, at least five different types being recognised, each capable of more minute subdivision, the stars are, in the main, composed of elements similar to those existing in the sun; and, in Professor Newcomb's words, 'as the sun contains most of the elements found on the earth and few or no others, we may say that earth and stars seem to be all made out of like matter.' It is, of course, impossible to say what unknown elements may exist in the stars; but at least it is certain that many substances quite familiar to us, such as iron, magnesium, calcium, hydrogen, oxygen, and carbon, are present in their constitution. Indeed, our own sun, in spite of its overwhelming importance to ourselves is to be regarded, relatively to the stellar multitudes, as merely one star among many; nor, so far as can be judged, can it be considered by any means a star of the first class. There can be no doubt that, if removed to the average distance of first magnitude stars— thirty-three years light journey—our sun would be merely a common-place member of the heavenly host, far outshone by many of its fellow-suns. In all probability it would shine as about a fifth magnitude star, with suspicions of variability in its light.

There remains to be noted the fact that the sun is not to be regarded as a fixed centre, its fixity being only relative to the members of its own system. With all its planets and comets it is sweeping continually through space with a velocity of more than 1,000,000 miles in the twenty-four hours. This remarkable fact was first suspected by Sir William Herschel, who also, with that insight which was characteristic of his wonderful genius, saw, and was able roughly to apply, the method which would either confirm or disprove the suspicion.

The principle which lies at the bottom of the determination is in itself simple enough, though its application is complicated in such a manner as to render the investigation a very difficult one. A wayfarer passing up the centre of a street lighted on both sides by lamps will see that the lamps in front of him appear to open out and separate from one another as he advances, while those that he is leaving behind him have an opposite motion, appearing to close in upon one another. Now, with regard to the solar motion, if the case were absolutely simple, the same effect would be produced upon the stars among which we are moving; that is to say, were the stars absolutely fixed, and our system alone in motion among them, there would appear to be a general thinning out or retreating of the stars from the point towards which the sun is moving, and a corresponding crowding together of them towards the point, directly opposite in the heavens, from which it is receding. In actual fact the case is not by any means so simple, for the stars are not fixed; they have motions of their own, some of them enormously greater than the motion of the sun. Thus the apparent motion caused by the advance of our system is masked to a great extent by the real motion of the stars. It is plain, however, that the perspective effect of the sun's motion must really be contained in the total motion of each star, or, in other words, that each star, along with its own real motion, must have an apparent motion which is common to all, and results from our movement through space. If this common element can be disentangled from the individual element, the proper motion of each star, then the materials for the solution of the problem will be secured. It has been found possible to effect this disentanglement, and the results of all those who have attempted the problem are, all things considered, in remarkably close agreement.

Herschel's application of his principle led him to the conclusion that there was a tendency among the stars to widen out from the constellation Hercules, and to crowd together towards the opposite constellation of Argo Navis in the southern hemisphere, and the point which he fixed upon as the apex of the sun's path was near the star Lambda Herculis. Subsequent discussions of the problem have confirmed, to a great extent, his rough estimate, which was derived from a comparatively small number of stars. So far as general direction was concerned, he was entirely right; the conclusion which he reached as to the exact point towards which the motion is directed has, however, been slightly modified by the discussion of a much larger number of stars, and it is now considered that the apex of the solar journey 'is in the general direction of the constellation Lyra, and perhaps near the star Vega, the brightest of that constellation' (Newcomb, 'The Stars,' p. 91). There are but few stars more beautiful and interesting than Vega; to its own intrinsic interest must now be added that arising from the fact that each successive night we look upon it we have swept more than 1,000,000 miles nearer to its brilliant globe, and that with every year we have lessened, by some 400,000,000 miles, the distance that divides us from it. There can surely be no thought more amazing than this! It seems to gather up and bring to a focus all the other impressions of the vastness of celestial distances and periods. So swift and ceaseless a motion, and yet the gulfs that sever us from our neighbours in space are so huge that a millennium of such inconceivable travelling makes no perceptible change upon the face of the heavens! There rise other thoughts to the mind. Towards what goal may our world and its companions be voyaging under the sway of the mighty ruler of the system, and at the irresistible summons of those far-off orbs which distance reduces to the mere twinkling points of light that in man's earliest childlike thought were but lamps hung out by the Creator to brighten the midnight sky for his favourite children? What strange chances may be awaiting sun and planet alike in those depths of space towards which we are rushing with such frightful speed? Such questions remain unanswered and unanswerable. We are as ignorant of the end of our journey, and of the haps that may attend it, as we are helpless in the grasp of the forces that compel and control it.